BILL AND *THE MARY ANN SHAUGHNESSY*

CATHERINE COOKSON

BILL AND *THE MARY ANN SHAUGHNESSY*

DOUBLEDAY

LONDON · NEW YORK · TORONTO · SYDNEY · AUCKLAND

TRANSWORLD PUBLISHERS LTD
61–63 Uxbridge Road, London W5 5SA

TRANSWORLD PUBLISHERS (AUSTRALIA) PTY LTD
15–23 Helles Avenue, Moorebank, NSW 2170

TRANSWORLD PUBLISHERS (NZ) LTD
Cnr Moselle and Waipareira Aves,
Henderson, Auckland

DOUBLEDAY CANADA LTD
105 Bond Street, Toronto, Ontario M5B 1Y3

Published 1991 by Doubleday
a division of Transworld Publishers Ltd

British Library Cataloguing in Publication Data
Cookson, Catherine 1906–
Bill and the Mary Ann Shaughnessy
I. Title
823.914 [J]

ISBN 0-385-40163-9

Typeset in Century Schoolbook by
Chippendale Type Ltd., Otley, West Yorkshire.
Printed and bound in Great Britain by
Mackays of Chatham PLC, Chatham, Kent

To Bill

Who, with me, wishes painful retribution to all those who train his breed to kill.

Foreword

We bought the boat in 1956 and christened her *The Mary Ann Shaughnessy* after the heroine of my Mary Ann stories; and over a period of ten years we spent many interesting hours on her. I say interesting, not happy: whereas my husband loved rivers and locks and was a good swimmer, Bill and I hated the locks and, what was more, neither of us could swim.

All the incidents on the rivers I describe actually did happen to some extent, except meeting the baddies. Yet we did come up with a very fine yacht, and I rammed her, and her owner was anything but pleased.

I wrote this story in 1960, and, as was many another, it was pushed into a cupboard. However, on coming across it recently, it revived our trips to the Cam; so, I hope you enjoy them more than I did.

Catherine Cookson

PART ONE

1

The three boys and the dog stood on the quay at Banham's boatyard in Cambridge and looked again at the boat that was to be their home for the next two weeks, and the boys' excitement held them speechless. The boat was named *The Mary Ann Shaughnessy*. She was a twenty-six foot cabin cruiser, white painted up to her super-structure which was a shining brown, except for her flat roof which was painted cream. She was front drive, the wheel very much like that of a car steering-wheel, more so because it was at seat-level height. The cockpit was about six feet in length and held the engine encased in a box, and seats all round. The main cabin was eight feet long, with a double and a single berth, which formed a comfortable lounge in the day-time. There was a small sideboard at the head of one bunk, and a half wardrobe at the head of the other, and a rack for books and papers ran all around the cabin.

The galley was only about five feet long and held a dinette with seats at either side. Opposite was a door which led to a lavatory and wash-basin, and next to it there was a good-sized sink with a pump above it, and to the right, above the draining-board, a calor gas ring and grill. One step led out of the galley into the back cockpit which was made up of lockers with only a small space in which to stand. From a flagpole attached to the middle of her transom flew the red ensign, and on each side of her high pointed bows she carried her name proudly on a varnished board.

She was a smart little lady. And that's what Mr Harrison, the storekeeper, said as he came up behind the boys, startling them for a moment. 'Yes, she's worth admiring. She may not be young any more but she's a smart little lady, and I hope you treat her as such.'

'Oh yes, yes, sir.' Jonathan Crawford moved his head deferentially to the man who had been so helpful to them since their arrival in the yard a few hours ago, and he said, 'We'll take care of her.'

'You'd better, boy, else I wouldn't like to be you when you face the owners . . . whether they are friends of your family or not. As I said a short time ago, it's a surprise to me that Mr and Mrs Cookson have let you have her, nothing short of a miracle in fact.'

Jonathan Crawford, looking at the storekeeper, endorsed his remark in his mind. It was indeed nothing short of a miracle that his Uncle Tom had lent his boat to them, and he still couldn't quite take in the fact that they were about to take her up the Cambridge rivers. For the first time he was glad that their trip abroad had fallen through.

If things had gone as planned the whole Crawford family would now have been in Norway, but his sister Lorna had to go and catch chicken-pox on the second day of the holidays; and if this wasn't bad enough she had to give them to young Jessica. After the wailing had died down somewhat his mother had almost caused a civil war by suggesting it would be a good thing for him and Malcolm to hob-nob with the girls in the hope that they might catch it too, for, as she said, they would have to get it some time and far better make one big job of it.

It might have been better from her point of view but not from theirs. The suggestion had driven him and Malcolm to camp out in the summerhouse. If they were to get chickenpox, all right, but to go asking for it, oh no. They were both loud in their protests. And so they had collected their meals from the kitchen and isolated themselves from the house. But not from Joe, Malcolm's friend from next door, and certainly not from their dog, Bill; 'that fellow', as his father had said, could be acting as a carrier for he spent his time racing between the girls' room and the summerhouse.

It was when their spirits were very low and they were toying with the idea of going camping, even when the weather forecast said rain, that Uncle Tom had phoned. Would the boys like to take a holiday on *The Mary Ann Shaughnessy*?

When the excitement had died down just the slightest, their father had almost put a spanner in the works by saying with loud finality, 'Well, if you go you take "that fellow" with you, mind.'

'That fellow' was a brindle bull terrier, a battle-scarred bull terrier, and it was only through the tenacity of the boys and the pleading of the girls that Bill was alive at all. In fact, he was practically under sentence of death at this moment, for if the postman took the case up Mr Crawford said that would be the last straw.

The trouble with Bill was that he loved people and liked to make their acquaintance, unless of course they happened to be carrying a stick and were unwise enough to wave it about. Only the members of his family were exempted from this peculiar aversion – he even allowed them to throw sticks for him to fetch. But whereas Bill loved humans he wholeheartedly hated the male members of his own species, no matter what breed, and when meeting up with them he would do his best to separate their bodies, long, tall, or short, from their heads. Over the years this weakness of Bill's had not only taken Mr Crawford into court, had not only cost him quite a deal of money, had not only very often filled his days and nights with worry, when Bill was on the rampage, but had lost him and the whole family a number of friends and created for them a good many enemies . . . But no-one could ever accuse Bill of being discourteous to a lady dog.

The boys protested vehemently that Bill would be unmanageable on a boat, but it got them nowhere. The ultimatum stood: they took 'that fellow' or they didn't go.

And then there was Joe from next door. The Taggarts came from the North and had been neighbours of the Crawfords for only six months. At first there had been Mr and Mrs Taggart and Grandma Taggart, then Mrs Taggart walked out one day and didn't return. Being a salesman, Mr Taggart was away most of the time, and Joe was left to the mercy of his grandmother, whom he didn't like. So Joe spent a great deal of his time in the Crawfords' house with Malcolm, who had become his best friend.

Malcolm Crawford was fourteen and short for his age, but he was thick-set and sturdy, whereas Joe, who was of the same age and about the same height, was as thin as a rake, which made him look younger than Malcolm. But both of them looked years younger than Jonathan, because Jonathan who was fifteen was already five foot six. So it was that when the three of them were together it was Jonathan who took the lead, and he was addressed as the leader, as now by Mr Harrison.

'Well,' he said, 'you've got your food aboard, you know where everything is. . . But mind what I told you about being careful with the calor gas. Always see it's turned off at the drum every time you've finished with the stove. And be especially careful when lighting the gas in the cockpit. You've got two spare gallons of petrol underneath the tank there and if you should spill any when you're filling her up again you just need a match to it and *whoof!* You'll be keeping company with the swans.'

When they all laughed, Bill, who had been sitting quietly by Malcolm's feet, dived away and raced in a circle around the trees.

'What's struck him?' asked Mr Harrison, as he watched the tufts of grass flying from Bill's rear paws.

'Bill! Bill! Here! Come! Stay! Bill! *Bill!*' As

15

Malcolm yelled at Bill, Jonathan said on a sigh, 'Oh, it's his way of laughing, sir. If we all laugh together he does that; and when it happens in the house . . . ' He left the sentence unfinished and Mr Harrison chuckled and said, 'Yes, I see what you mean.'

Suddenly pulling himself to a standstill, Bill stood panting for a moment, his broad chest pumping in and out; then quite sedately he walked towards the group, his mouth open and his tongue dripping saliva.

'Has he been on a boat before?' asked Mr Harrison, looking down at Bill, and Malcolm replied, 'No, sir, never.'

'Get aboard, Joe,' said Jonathan now, 'and I'll hand him to you. And mind, hang on to him.'

'Hang on to him, you say,' said Joe in a voice that was distinctly different from Jonathan's and Malcolm's, and even Mr Harrison's, because of its North-country inflection. 'What if he decides to jump overboard, does the order still hold good?'

'Yes,' said Jonathan firmly. 'Whatever he does you hang on to him until we get under way.'

'Well, don't forget you told me to. Come on, boy. Come on, boy.' As Joe jumped into the cockpit and held his arms up for Bill, Mr Harrison said, 'Now why don't you let him jump aboard himself; he'll have to do it.'

'He won't, sir; we've tried for the last half-an-hour to get him to jump. He'll jump *off* but he won't jump *on*.'

'Well, in that case I think I'd keep him in the cabin until you get off. Mr Hawtrey gave you a trial trip, didn't he?'

16

'Yes, sir,' said Jonathan.

'And you feel quite confident in taking her out?'

'Yes, yes, I think I'll be all right. I'll be better after a little practice; there'll be nothing to it tomorrow.'

'Ah-ah! Don't get too confident all at once. Anybody can steer a boat when there's nothing fore or aft, or to port or starboard, but you'll meet quite a lot of obstacles on the river, and so remember what I've told you.'

'Yes, I'll remember. And thank you very much, you've been very kind.'

'Oh, that's nothing. Now you all get aboard and I'll hold your stern until you get her bows out, just in case you should touch the boat alongside there.'

Malcolm pursed his lips and made a face as he said, 'Coo! We'd better not start off by doing that; she's a marvellous-looking boat, isn't she?'

'Yes, she's a very nice boat,' said Mr Harrison. 'It's the first time I've seen her down this way. She's sea-going and must have come round from Lowestoft.'

'And he looks like a real captain,' said Malcolm under his breath now as they turned their gaze to a man in a peak cap, blue brass-buttoned coat and white duck trousers, who had just come up on deck.

'Yes, he does, doesn't he?' Mr Harrison was whispering back and laughing. 'But you know the saying, it takes more than a peak cap to ride a storm.' He pushed at Malcolm, and Malcolm grinned at him. Then, seeing that Jonathan was

17

waiting impatiently for him to get aboard, he dropped down into the cockpit and Jonathan, having followed, switched on the petrol, then started her up and took the wheel.

When the bow rope had been neatly coiled on the foredeck Jonathan swung the bows gently past the stern of the big white boat ahead, and made for the middle of the river.

'All right?' Mr Harrison's voice shouted now. 'Away you go! But take it gently at first, and remember what I've told you.'

'Yes, sir. Goodbye, Mr Harrison,' Malcolm called. And Joe's muffled shout came from the cabin, 'Ta-rah! Mr Harrison.'

Jonathan too called, 'Goodbye, Mr Harrison. And thank you once again.' But he did not look at the old man, for his whole attention was centred at the moment on his steering.

Then they were in the middle of the river and under way, and as they neared the gasworks Joe shouted from the cabin, 'Can I come out now, he's going mad?'

'Wait till we get a little further on,' Jonathan called back.

'He'll have the place torn to bits, mind I'm tellin' you.'

'Oh, come on then,' called Jonathan, and the next moment Bill came into the cockpit knocking Malcolm flying over the engine box. 'Grab him!' cried Jonathan as he saw Bill make a lightning jump for the locker that formed a step on the starboard side of the boat. But there was no need to grab him for Bill didn't jump overboard; instead, his head hanging over the gunwale he

18

looked down at the frothing waves arrowing from the bows. He looked at them for quite a minute before turning his ugly scarred face round to the boys, and such was the expression on it that they were forced to laugh.

'He's flabbergasted,' said Joe.

'If it'll keep him quiet let's pray he'll remain flabbergasted,' said Malcolm.

They had now come up with a mass of swans forming a white sheet across the river, and not one of them seemed disposed to move until Bill let out a series of excited barks. But when two of the swans, keeping pace with the boat, hissed up at him, he sat back on his haunches in surprise, and again turned his gaze to the boys as if to ask them what they thought of that.

'When do I take her?' asked Joe, now thrusting his thin face in front of Malcolm and towards Jonathan.

'I thought we'd settled that,' said Jonathan. 'You can have a turn at her when we get through the locks.'

'Locks! Both of them?' said Joe on a high note.

'Both of them,' said Jonathan flatly. 'Remember what Mr Harrison said.'

'Oh, I think he's an old duffer,' said Joe. 'I bet he talks like that to everybody. It's nothing really taking a motor cruiser out. It isn't like a sailing boat; anybody can work these. It tells you that in the catalogues.'

Malcolm gave Joe a sly dig in the ribs, and accompanied it by a warning glance. The glance said, don't get Jonathan's back up.

Malcolm liked Joe. He was different from any

19

other of his friends. He was funny and made you laugh, and he was kind and willing to share anything he had, but he had the unfortunate knack of getting people's backs up with the things he said, and he wouldn't take a hint. He went into the attack again, saying, 'You know, I think we should get a sort of rota out, turn an' turn about. What d'you say?'

Jonathan said, 'I say shut up.' Then after a pause he added, on a laugh, 'But I think you're right about a rota. We'll all have to muck in with the work so until we get through the locks we'll just make your job the easy one of seeing to Bill there.'

'Aw, go on.' Joe slapped his hand at Jonathan and cast a disdainful glance on Bill, where he was lying on the locker, his head on his paws, his little eyes darting from one to the other, waiting for a sign or an inflection of the voice that he could take as an order. And Joe cried, 'I had him when we were leaving, that was enough. Let's be fair, turn an' turn about with him an' all.'

'He's in your charge, Joe, until we get through the locks. So that's settled.'

'Heck!' said Joe. 'It's victimization, that's what it is.'

Jonathan had to look over the side of the boat so that the others wouldn't see him smiling. It was hard to look at and listen to Joe and not laugh, but Joe only needed a little encouragement and then anything could happen. He was like Bill in a way.

Inwardly Jonathan was a little perturbed about

getting through the locks ahead. From the conversation he'd had on the phone with his uncle he had gathered that there always seemed to be a breeze blowing across Baitsbite, the first lock, and his uncle had advised him to turn at right angles and steer straight from the middle of the river to the bank, then to turn her sharply to starboard so that the stern would swing close to the bank. This, he had said, would give the boys time to get off and keep her steady with the bow and stern ropes.

All these instructions were passing through Jonathan's mind when, half-an-hour later, on rounding a bend, he saw the lock. His stomach muscles contracting just a little, he said in a clipped tone, which he imagined the captain of a liner might use when giving his orders, 'Immediately I get her bows near the bank, Malcolm, you jump off and play out the rope . . . Joe, you get on to the aft deck now and have the rope ready, but see it's well fastened to the cleat first. And when her stern comes round jump on to the bank and hang on to the rope . . . Now mind—' he cast a quick glance towards Joe and nodded sternly at him '— you hang on to her. The back's the hardest to hold, so remember.'

'Aye, aye, sir.' Laughing, Joe ran through the cabin, and his running was the signal for Bill to jump off the seat and follow him.

As the sound of a scuffle came to Jonathan he yelled, 'Stop acting the goat, Joe! Shut the door on him.'

'Get in! Stop going daft. Get in will you!' Joe's

voice came through the cabin, ending sarcastically, 'Shut the door on him, he says, just like that!' There followed a bang, and the next minute Bill had re-entered the cockpit and jumped on to the driving-seat behind Jonathan, who was standing gripping the wheel as he turned the boat away from the middle of the river and the roar of the weir, which lay to his right, and headed her bows for the bank.

A sense of achievement came to Jonathan when he watched Malcolm jump smartly from the high bows on to the bank, the long rope loosely running through his hands. So far, so good. But lost in the thrill of the moment, he was just that fraction too late in swinging the wheel to starboard, and *The Mary Ann*, not having enough way on her and caught by the wind blowing down river, seemed bent on presenting her stern to the lock gates. Just in time, Jonathan, remembering how Mr Hawtrey had reversed her, pressed the lever hard back and pushed up the throttle to its full extent, shouting as he did so, 'Slacken the rope, Malcolm, I'm reversing her!'

Malcolm slackened the rope; then Jonathan, putting the lever into the forward position, again brought her bows to the bank, but this time he swung the wheel round to starboard almost as she touched. And now he actually felt her answering his orders. Glancing over the side he saw the stern about a yard from the bank and Joe in the act of jumping off, and when he saw him land on the bank he again thought, so far so good. But once more he had counted without the wind and the fact that *The Mary Ann Shaughnessy*, being single-engined and with her long shaft running through to the propeller, was inclined to skip to starboard at the slightest beckoning of a breeze. It was with irritation, mixed with consternation, that Jonathan now saw the stern moving rapidly from the bank and, what was more, that fool of a Joe obeying his order to the letter.

Being fundamentally of a tenacious character, Joe imagined that his strength could hold the boat. The next minute he was proved wrong, and with a yell he hit the water.

'Jonathan! Jonathan! He's fallen in!' Malcolm shouted, his laughter lost now in concern.

Jonathan, leaning over the side, saw Joe's head and arms emerging from some reeds near the bank and he bawled at him, 'Get out of that quick in case her stern comes in again.'

But it was slowly that Joe pulled himself up on to the bank again, and he was still standing spluttering and speechless when Malcolm called excitedly, 'The lock-keeper's opening the gates, Jonathan! He's opening the gates!' And Jonathan, aiming to keep calm, cried, 'Well, we can't get in unless he does, can we?'

When the man on the lockside waved them in Jonathan called to Malcolm, 'Throw the rope on board and get along there, both of you.'

Backing *The Mary Ann* into the middle of the river again, Jonathan straightened her out and the next minute she was making for the lock, her bows wavering slightly as Jonathan tried to guide her dead centre, while his mind repeated the instructions . . . *plenty of way on her*

23

until you pass the gates, then sharp into reverse; then into neutral, but leave the engine running. He swallowed deeply twice as her bows passed the big black wooden gates and when he saw the other two gates looming up only a short distance away he felt a wave of panic run through him, but automatically he followed the instructions and his charge came to rest in the lock with only a slight loss of dignity as her bows hit one lock wall while her trim stern bumped the other.

'Hold her by the deck rail.' The lock-keeper's unemotional voice gave the order to the boys, and they grabbed the rail and slowly drew her towards the left-hand side wall.

Bill, who had been standing with quivering body on the far locker during all this, now saw his chance of freedom, if only for a short while, so with one long spring he made the lock quay.

'Oh no, you don't!' Hauling him aboard again, Jonathan dumped him on the far locker and admonished him sternly. 'Now I'm telling you: stay! STAY!'

The lock-keeper came down the quay again and, surveying Joe, with a rueful twist to his lips said, 'You're wet, aren't you?'

Feeling very uncomfortable and shivering now, Joe glanced up at the burly figure and after a moment he remarked caustically, 'No, I'm not wet, I'm just sweatin'.'

The lock-keeper narrowed his eyes at him, then walked on, with the remark, 'You'll learn.' And Joe, looking along to Malcolm, who was shaking with laughter, hissed, 'Learn, he said. Not if I

24

know it. Hang on to the rope I was told, and don't leave go.'

Jonathan put his head above the hatchway, and he, too, was laughing as he looked towards Joe. Then glancing towards the quay to where there was a little store with soft drinks advertised, he said, 'What about a bottle or two?'

'Good idea,' said Malcolm, and at this Jonathan said 'Well, slip across and get them. I'll hold her until you get back.'

As Malcolm stepped on to the quay Jonathan turned round to Bill and said firmly, 'Stay!' And Bill stayed. He stayed until he saw a lady with four legs descending a short flight of steps in the distance. She was a boxer and it was evident that she had only recently had a family. The perfume of her came to Bill and brought him to his hind legs with his front paws on the gunwale, and there he stood in lip-dripping admiration as he watched her come steadily towards him.

At heart Bill was a gentleman, and all members of the opposite sex, no matter what breed or type, aroused in him chivalrous admiration. Following the pattern of his usual approach that such meetings demanded, he said 'How do you do?' with a number of quick sniffs and the lady, still some distance away, responded graciously ... at least she had all intentions of so doing, but at that moment the quiver of excitement that was filling Bill's body turned, in a flash, to a feeling not only of apprehension but of real fear. The sound that caused this was equivalent in his mind to a hundred lavatory chains being pulled at once. But he hadn't time to ascertain the cause

25

because before his petrified gaze he actually saw the lady rising in the air. It wasn't until he realized that the lady was stationary and that it was himself who was sinking that he threw aside all gentlemanly restraint to the wind, and after making one fruitless effort to jump the ever-widening space between the gunwale and the top of the quay, he turned and made a wild dash through the cabin to the aftdeck, and there the same sight met his gaze, only worse. The water was disappearing with a deafening roar and he and the boat were sinking, down, down, down. Again he crashed through the cabin and into the cockpit and now he was forced to cry for help. He did it in a series of wild, ear-splitting howls before trying to make his escape through one of the cabin windows. This being fruitless, he stared for a sickening moment at the black walls of the lock, running with water and slime. Then swiftly returning to the cockpit, and seeing Jonathan dropping down on to the locker, he hurled himself at him and begged for protection.

'Stop it, you mad fool! Get down! Get in there. Stop it! Stop it!' When at last, after a struggle, Jonathan had him safely locked in the cabin, Joe shouted down from the quay, 'Well, how did you like it? You wouldn't believe me, would you?'

The lock-keeper was pressing his back against the huge lever now which was opening half of the fore lockgates, then with his long pole he pushed the other half back into place, after which he called, 'Come on. Come on.'

'Get aboard!' shouted Jonathan, and when the boys had lowered themselves down from the roof on to the narrow deck, he opened the throttle and gently eased the boat forward. And then they were through and into the river again, and for a moment they were quiet; the whole boat was quiet because now there was no sound of rampaging from the cabin.

Jonathan straightened himself, then inhaling deeply he seated himself before the wheel, and casting a glance at Joe, said, 'I wouldn't stand there, I'd get those things off.'

'Why should I?' said Joe. 'We've got another lock to go through, haven't we?'

They all laughed and when Joe, saying, 'Wait for it!', opened the door into the cabin Bill shot between his legs, raced round the engine and back again, and after looking from Jonathan to Malcolm jumped up on to the side locker and lay down panting.

'You should just see this place,' called Joe. 'Coo! Take good care of *The Mary Ann Shaughnessy* your uncle said. If he wanted that done he should have got someone to take care of *him*. There won't be anything left inside by the time we get back.'

'And that's what I'm afraid of,' said Jonathan under his breath to Malcolm, and Malcolm, looking lovingly at Bill, said, 'Give him a chance, it's all strange to him. He'll settle down, you'll see. It's strange to us an' all. You must admit, Jonathan, it is.'

Jonathan didn't admit it, not openly, but inside himself he knew that it was very strange indeed, perhaps more strange to him than to the other two because he felt responsible. He was in charge of *The Mary Ann Shaughnessy* and for a moment,

27

but only for a moment, he wished he wasn't.

'How far is it to the next lock?' Malcolm asked, some time later.

'I'm not quite sure,' replied Jonathan. 'What we should have is the map laid out on top of the engine there.'

'It'd blow away in this wind,' said Joe.

'We can put something on the corners,' said Malcolm, diving into the cabin and returning a moment later with the long map. 'There,' he said, bending over it. 'Where are we now? Oh yes; we're near the village of Horningsea, over there to the right.'

'There's a lot of squiggles in the river before we get to the next lock,' put in Joe now; and Malcolm pushed him as he repeated, 'Squiggles! They're bends. There's nothing much until we come to Clayhythe and The Bridge Hotel; then there's the Cambridge Boat and Sailing Club. That should be good to see, shouldn't it?'

But when they passed the Cambridge Boat and Sailing Club the boys didn't remark on it much, for an incident prior to their arrival there had filled them with indignation. They had been moving along just to the right of the middle of the river when they were all startled by a double hoot from the port side, and Malcolm, jumping up on the locker and bringing a groan from Bill as he trod on the end of his tail, shouted to Jonathan, 'It's a boat passing us.' In the meantime Joe had dashed through the cabin to the stern, and when he returned a minute later he gasped at Jonathan, 'It's that big boat from the yard,

28

The Night Star, you know, and she's gallopin'.'

Jonathan did not raise his eyebrows and scathingly repeat, 'Galloping!' but immediately gave way by turning the wheel sharply to starboard. Casting a glance to his left he now saw the high bows of the boat as it overtook them at speed.

'Coo! He's rocking us,' said Joe. And he *was* rocking them. Instead of keeping well to their port side the big boat was hogging the middle of the river and, when he was past, his wash sent back large waves and *The Mary Ann Shaughnessy* bounced and jibbed as they pushed her nearer to the starboard bank.

'Did you see that?' cried Joe.

'Courtesy of the river!' exclaimed Malcolm indignantly. 'That's what they said to us back at the yard; "Go slow when you're passing boats".'

'They meant stationary ones,' said Jonathan; then he added tersely, 'but who does he think he is, anyway?'

'And look there!' cried Joe, pointing to a notice. 'Dead slow while passing the boats moored at the club. And look at the speed he's going.'

'He has slowed down a bit,' said Jonathan now.

'You've said it . . . a bit.'

'And now here's more trouble,' said Joe. 'Look at those two sailing boats coming at us. And they're going some an' all.'

Both he and Malcolm knelt on the locker with Bill squeezed between them and watched the approach of the sailing craft. And Jonathan noted their approach too, and with some trepidation. The boats, their red sails gleaming, were tacking, and from different sides of the river.

29

For a moment he didn't know what to do. Then he remembered what Mr Hawtrey had said with regard to sail: 'Give way entirely. And when in doubt do nothing; leave it to them.' And this is what he did now, and the boats, seeming to miss his bows by inches, glided skilfully past, bringing exclamations of admiration from the boys.

They were nearing a sharp bend of the river now, and Malcolm, looking at the map, said, 'Bottisham lock must be round this corner. But look; there's a red flag out there and a notice up.'

'What does it say?' asked Jonathan. 'Can you see?'

'Not from here. We should have binoculars, shouldn't we?'

'Well, as we haven't, get up on the roof and use your eyes.'

'It says,' shouted Malcolm, ' "Danger. River work in progress". And Jonathan, I can see the tops of boats coming out of the lock.'

'They won't get very far without their bottoms,' laughed Joe.

'Funny! Funny!' shouted Malcolm down at him. ' . . . And Jonathan, I can see *The Night Star* waiting to go into the lock.'

'Well, we don't want to go in with him,' said Jonathan flatly, as he slowed down.

But they had to go into the lock with *The Night Star*. After having to hug the bank to let the outcoming boats pass, and having watched the big steady bulk of *The Night Star* going smoothly into the lock, they were then waved forward by the lock-keeper.

'Now mind,' whispered Jonathan fiercely as he

gripped the wheel and brought *The Mary Ann*'s bows in line with the mouth of the lock. 'Don't let's have any more trouble with HIM. One of you hang on to Bill.'

'But who'll hold the boat?' asked Joe quickly.

'If one of you is on the quay I can keep her off from down below. I think I see rubber tyres hanging down the walls; they should keep her clear. But the main thing is, keep that fellow from going berserk.' Jonathan thumbed towards Bill, who answered the gesture with a pained look.

Following the same procedure that he had used when entering the previous lock Jonathan now found to his dismay that procedures had to be adapted to circumstances. *The Night Star* was taking up more than half the length of the lock and so not allowing him the space in which to act according to the book, so, having gone in with 'way on', he did not reverse quickly enough to bring *The Mary Ann Shaughnessy* to a stop before she reached the stern of *The Night Star*.

'Here! What you think you're up to? Slow up! Slow up! can't you?'

As *The Mary Ann*'s bows bumped against the stern of *The Night Star* the huge figure of a man in a jersey with a close-cut bullet-shaped head came round the deck and, with his foot, thrust angrily at the bows below him.

'Haven't you got eyes?' He was bending over now and glaring through the open windscreen at Jonathan, and Jonathan replied apologetically, 'I'm sorry.'

'Sorry be damned! You should have practised on a bike and learned to steer.'

31

'I said I was sorry.' Jonathan's voice was no longer quiet.

The man picked up a short boat-hook now and pushed it against *The Mary Ann*'s bows to ward her off, and as he did so there came a low growl from Bill as he jumped out of Malcolm's hold and sprang on to the seat below the windscreen, where, standing on his hind legs, he now began to bark furiously at the man on the stern above him.

With his arms tightly around Bill, Malcolm shouted through the open window, 'Please, sir! Would you mind not holding that stick . . . I mean that boat-hook.'

'What?' the man shouted. 'What do you say?'

'The boat-hook. Our dog doesn't like sticks.'

'Oh! He doesn't, eh?' The man looked at the boat-hook in his hand. 'Well, that's a pity, isn't it? Strikes me he needs training.'

'Please!' said Malcolm again. 'He'll stop barking if you put it down.'

'And what if I don't?'

'What is it, Sloper?' The man wearing the peak cap and the blue reefer coat had come out of the wheelhouse. His voice was different from the other man's, quieter, more refined.

'Oh, nothing,' said the man Sloper. 'Just that ugly mug's barking because I've got the hook in my hand. They want me to put it down.'

'Well, put it down.'

'What?'

'Put it down.'

'Oh!' Sloper put down the hook; then slanting his gaze at the owner, moved slowly away out of

32

sight, and the man in the peak cap smiled as he looked at Bill and said, 'He looks a stout fellow. I wouldn't like to meet up with him in the dark.'

Malcolm smiled slowly; and Jonathan smiled; and Joe on the quay smiled.

'What's his name?' the man now asked.

'Bill, sir,' said Malcolm.

'Very appropriate.' The man nodded; then said, 'Your first trip on the river?' He was bending slightly forward and looking past Malcolm to Jonathan now, and Jonathan nodded and said, 'Yes, sir. We haven't got used to the ropes yet. I'm sorry I bumped your bows.'

'Oh! You bumped her, did you? Well, I didn't even notice.' He looked over the side. 'Not a scratch.'

'She's a beautiful boat, sir,' said Malcolm, looking up at the radio mast.

'I think so too.' The man smiled, then turned away when, the lock-keeper having drawn up the sluice gates, the boats began their gradual fall to the level of the next part of the river.

Bill just couldn't believe it, but of course he should have known that once they passed those black gates they'd be dropped into a well. It made no difference that he had his two masters with him now: he didn't like wells any better than he liked men with sticks. As he leapt from Malcolm's hold into the cabin Jonathan's hand flashed out, but missed him. When he reached the small well of the aft deck and stood on his hind legs with his paws on the locker and barked furiously, he heard Joe's voice calling down to him, 'It's all right, you idiot,' but he found no reassurance in it; instead he turned to make another sortie, and collided head on with Malcolm. Then he was hauled on to the bunk and had the indignity of being lain upon, while Malcolm's two hands gripped his collar. This sort of tackle wasn't fair, but he stopped his barking and lay trembling, one white-rimmed eye turned upwards to that awful moving black wall outside the window.

When presently the black wall gave way to green fields and blue skies he was allowed to stand up. After shaking himself, he looked Malcolm in the eye and told him he bore him no ill will, then went quietly out of the cabin and took up his position on the seat he had chosen for his own.

They were now travelling in the wake of *The Night Star*, but it was getting further and further away from them, and Jonathan, his eyes on it, remarked, 'He was rather decent.'

'Yes,' agreed Malcolm; 'he seems a very nice man. That other fellow is likely just one of his crew.'

'There were two others besides him,' said Joe. 'A little fellow with bandy legs—' he gave an imitation of what the man looked like '—an' another bloke, who could be King Kong's cousin.'

'The owner called that big-mouthed fellow Sloper,' said Malcolm.

'There used to be a sauce called Sloper,' said Joe musingly. 'I remember when I used to go to me grannie's when I was little, she always had it on the table in a three-gill bottle. Ally Sloper's sauce.'

Malcolm and Jonathan began to chuckle, low

sounds at first, which gradually grew until they were doubled up with laughter. They often found that Joe's reminiscing had this effect on them; it was the odd way he came out with things. He could be very funny about his grannie, although he disliked her so much.

Jonathan's laughter had a strong element of relief in it. He had brought *The Mary Ann Shaughnessy* through two locks, and under difficult circumstances which had nothing to do with either wind or weather, because anybody who had the choice would pick a storm in preference to the rumpus that Bill could create. Yes, he felt he had achieved something and could rightfully feel that he was, in a way, the master of *The Mary Ann Shaughnessy*.

2

They spent their first night up a little creek, leading to Burwell Lode, which could be entered through a lock and which led to a bird sanctuary. Bill had not been slow to voice his feelings at the sight of yet another lock and the boys had some difficulty in convincing him that they had no intention of going through it. There was only one other boat in the creek and it was canvassed up and evidently not in use. So, with the rond anchors safely dug into the bank, they had, after a great deal of commotion, their first meal aboard, which consisted of sausages and fried tomatoes, new bread, currant buns, and a wedge each of the large fruit cake that Mrs Crawford had packed for them.

And then came the business of washing-up, and as only two could stand in the galley with any degree of comfort the operation was slow and threaded with much nudging, pushing and laughter.

Following this, they looked at the map and plotted their journey for the next day, which took in The Royal Oak Hotel up the old West River, from where they were to phone home and reassure their parents that all was well.

When the light began to fade and a chilliness settled on the cabin, Joe suggested that they should light the Tilley lamp, but this was quickly decried by Jonathan, saying, 'We know nothing about that; we'd better leave it alone.'

'Oh, I can light a Tilley lamp,' said Joe.

'When did you light a Tilley lamp?' Malcolm asked, scathingly now. 'You say such daft things.'

'Daft nothing. I've lit a Tilley lamp dozens of times. Me grannie used to have one in her cottage when she lived right out on the fells near Hexham. She used to say it gave her warmth an' light at the same time, but Mam said she only lit it because she was too mean to burn coal.' Joe's face suddenly lost its perkiness and Jonathan, quick to notice this, and after exchanging a glance with Malcolm, said airily, 'Well, go ahead then, light it, as we're not supposed to use the electric lights too much in case of running down the battery.'

Joe remained silent as he went about the intricate business of lighting the lamp. But when the job was completed Malcolm's and Jonathan's praise brought him back to normal, and he exclaimed airily, 'Oh, there's nothin' to it.'

'Doesn't it look smashing!' said Malcolm, following Joe into the cabin, and Joe, placing the lamp on the sideboard, answered, 'It'll be smashing if Big Bill Hiccock decides to go mad.'

'Yes, that's a thought,' said Jonathan solemnly. 'We'd better keep him over on this side. Come on, boy. On to this bunk.'

But Bill, instead of jumping from one bunk to the other, put his two front paws on the floor, dragged his hind quarters lazily after them, and walked into the cockpit where he made a small whining sound, which brought an exclamation from both Jonathan and Malcolm at the same time. 'You've been!' they said.

But say what they might, Bill argued otherwise.

'Oh Lor! I'll have to take him out again,' said Jonathan now. 'Throw me my pullover. And I'd better put him on the lead in case we meet up with a car.'

'It's funny that,' said Joe; 'I've never heard any cars passing along this road. It's like the back of beyond. I don't think you need worry about him bumping into a car.'

'They sound like famous last words,' said Jonathan as he moved off into the gathering darkness. Cautiously, he guided Bill past the lock and on to the main road and to where, a little way along it, there was a lane leading down to a boathouse and an open space. It was here that Bill had rampaged shortly after they had berthed. Having reached this spot again, Jonathan let him off the lead, but when Bill decided to make an exploration in the rough growth at the end of the field Jonathan ran to prevent him, and it was as he did so that he noticed the white gleam of the boat moored a short distance away in the main river. It was almost at the same moment that the van turned into the lane, and stopped within a few yards of where Jonathan was crouched over Bill.

Then he felt Bill's bristles rising and his own ears pricked up at the sound of the voice coming to them from the roadway, saying, 'Hello, Duffy.

Everything all right?' for it was the unmistakable gruff voice of Sloper.

Another voice answered now, saying, 'Yes, right as rain. They were very obliging – killed two birds with one stone.'

'You don't say!' This was yet another voice, and it ended on a quiet laugh.

Jonathan remained crouched down, and gently stroked Bill's head. He saw the dark figures of the men go to the back of the van and slowly pull out some object which they proceeded to carry down to the boat. He couldn't make out what the object was, only that it must have been very heavy as it made Sloper gasp as he said, 'Seems too good to be true.' And the answering voice gasped also as it said, 'Well, seeing's believing, isn't it?'

Not until Jonathan thought they had reached the river bank did he move into the lane. He entered it at a spot just beyond the back of the van, and turning to glance at it he stopped dead in amazement and peered at the figure lying on the floor. He could just make out it was a man and he hadn't time to wonder if he were dead, or alive, when the man gave evidence of the latter by flinging his arm outwards and making a sound between a sigh and a groan. As Bill gave a low growl Jonathan heard footsteps approaching again, and he turned swiftly and made for the road. But his withdrawal wasn't noiseless, although he kept to the verge of the lane, and within a minute he heard a commotion behind him, and then the sound of running feet.

He was in the ditch with Bill held tightly to

him, one hand gripping his muzzle, when the men reached the road.

'Must have been dreaming,' said a low voice.

'Tell you I wasn't.' It was Sloper's voice.

'Could have been a fox, stray dog or anything. Come on.'

But Sloper did not come on right away.

Jonathan could hear him walking among the undergrowth. But at last there was silence and Jonathan, pulling himself and Bill up out of the ditch, ran pell-mell back to the boat and startled both Malcolm and Joe by diving straight at the Tilley lamp and turning it out.

'What's up with you?' Joe sat where Jonathan's entry had pushed him.

'I don't rightly know,' gasped Jonathan; 'but listen.' And he proceeded to tell them what had transpired, and when he had finished there was silence for a moment before Malcolm said, 'But the man in the van, was he hurt?'

'I've told you I don't know,' replied Jonathan; 'I had to get away.'

'Perhaps he was just asleep.'

'Don't talk like a nit, Malcolm,' said Joe scathingly. 'I bet you what you like he's been mugged.'

'And now you stop talking like a nit,' Jonathan said.

'Then what's all the fuss about?' asked Joe pointedly. 'You dashin' in here and putting out the light.'

'Well, I didn't want them to know we were round the corner; they might suspect, and rightly, that it was one of us who was snooping.'

'They likely know already,' said Malcolm.

'Somehow I doubt it,' replied Jonathan. 'But I wouldn't be surprised if they took a stroll around this way before long, so let's turn in, and should they come we could say we've been in bed for ages because we were tired with the trip.'

Five minutes later they were in their bunks, Malcolm and Joe in the double one, Jonathan in the single, with Bill curled up at his feet. And there they lay talking in whispers and waiting.

'Whatever the man Sloper is up to I don't think the owner would be in on it. Do you, Jonathan?' asked Malcolm.

'I shouldn't think so,' said Jonathan sleepily. 'He seemed such a decent sort.'

'Can't trust anybody. That's what me grannie's always sayin',' muttered Joe.

'Why do you always quote your grannie when you don't like her?' asked Malcolm now. 'Bet you love her deep down,' he added teasingly.

'Love me grannie?' said Joe slowly. 'I love her so much I wish she'd swallow a tin opener.'

The last thing Jonathan remembered before dropping off to sleep was the three of them spluttering with laughter.

Bill was uneasy; there were strange sounds all around him, and they weren't caused by the wind alone. He had dropped into a fitful doze, then woken up with the cold. He now gave a low growl as a water vole softly bumped the side of the boat. When an owl hooted as it flew overhead the points of his ears quivered. This sound was followed by a scurrying on the river bank and a peculiar squawking as if pheasants had been

41

disturbed. He lifted his head now and listened intently and growled a little louder. He felt a sense of uneasiness; things weren't right. He sat up straight and sniffed. There seemed to be strange movements all around him. He growled again, louder this time, then moved up the bunk and pushed against Jonathan with his muzzle.

Jonathan groaned, turned over, and, pushing Bill's face away, muttered thickly, 'Lie down, will you. Lie down.'

But Bill did not lie down. Picking his way to the bottom of the bunk again, he dropped on to the floor and sniffed at the door. A strong gust of wind rocked the boat, and then his head was brought upwards by the sound of rain pinging on the cabin roof. He turned his body round and walked through the cabin and into the galley, and here his uneasiness increased for there seemed to be movement under his feet. He was now experiencing the same sensation as when Jonathan sat at the wheel driving the boat, only now there was no noise with the movement. The curtains at the dinette window were not drawn and he jumped up on to the seat and looked out.

The squall of rain stopped as quickly as it began and the moon, coming out for a moment from behind thick scudding clouds, showed Bill a strange scene: what he should have been looking at was a green bank a few yards away across the narrow creek, but what he saw was a wide expanse of water seeming to stretch endlessly ahead. When the water suddenly gave place to trees, and a bank came rearing up to the window, he stepped back and fell on to the floor. The moon disappeared, the cabin was dark again and there were mutterings from the boys, a groan from Joe, a thick 'What was that?' from Malcolm, and a 'Where are you, Bill? Come on; lie down this minute!' from Jonathan.

'Whoof! Whoof! Whoof!' Bill spoke loudly. Standing on his hind legs, he pawed at Jonathan's shoulder. 'Whoof! Whoof! Whoof!'

'Oh, for crying out loud! Lie down, you idiot.'

'Perhaps he's cold,' muttered Malcolm sleepily.

'That's likely it,' mumbled Joe; 'I'm not very warm meself. Let him come in with us.'

'Whoof! Whoof! Whoof! Whoof!'

Jonathan sat up, rubbing the sleep from his eyes. His mind clearing, he switched on the light and blinked as he said, 'He doesn't bark for nothing.'

'Jonathan!' Joe was sitting bolt upright now. 'Do you feel something? We're . . . we're on the move.'

Within a second they had tumbled out of their bunks and were in the cockpit, and as if they had been dropped on to a strange planet they peered through the windscreen into the darkness. Then with a yell Jonathan tore at the press-studs on the awning, pulling it down as he cried, 'We're adrift!'

'We can't be,' said Malcolm. 'I hammered in the rond anchors.'

'Shut up, and wake up, man,' shouted Joe now. 'Can't you see we're loose in the main river . . . Oh heck!'

'Switch on the petrol, Joe,' ordered Jonathan now. 'And you, Malcolm, put her headlight on.'

As Jonathan tried to get the engine to start, the beam of light spreading over the water showed them that they were indeed in the middle of the river and being carried down broadside with the current.

'Won't she start?' cried Joe anxiously as he bent down by the side of Jonathan.

'No; she must be cold.'

'Try the starting handle.'

Without further ado Jonathan swung the starting handle and the engine ticked over for a moment, then lapsed into silence, and in the moment of quiet that followed Bill barked and Malcolm cried, 'Oh, shut up you!' Then pointing ahead, he gasped, 'She's making straight for the bank on the bend.'

'Well let's hope she sticks in the mud,' said Jonathan, 'else the Lord knows where we'll land.'

But the current took *The Mary Ann Shaughnessy* round the bend and once more they were in the middle of the river, and with the strong wind behind them they made crazy headway down it.

Jonathan, trying the self-starter again, pulled out the choke at the same time. The result was a quick throb from the engine, and an audible sigh of relief from each of them.

When Jonathan straightened her out he didn't know whether he was facing up or down river; all he wanted to do was to get her safely moored. But this was easier said than done because the silt was banked in places well out into the river. Time and again when he tried to steer her towards the dim outline of a bank her bows stuck in the mud. On the fifth attempt he brought her alongside a

44

high bank, and Joe, scrambling off with the bow rope in his hand, held her while Malcolm, from the deck, pulled in the stern with the boat-hook dug into the bank. Then, the engine shut off, Jonathan looked over the side to see Malcolm and Joe standing holding the ropes, and together they said the same things: 'Rond anchors.' And Joe added, 'We've got nothing to tie her to.'

Peering along the bank, Jonathan said, 'That looks like the stump of a willow. Pull her up a bit, but not too close in case there are roots sticking out.'

A few minutes later they had the bow rope securely tied to the willow stump, and Jonathan drove the round end of the boat-hook as far into the earth as he could, and to this they tied the stern rope.

Back on board, the boys, dropping on to the tumbled bunks, stared at each other. And when Joe's teeth began to chatter, Jonathan said, 'We'd better have a hot drink before we try to sort this out. I'll make it. You two get into bed. And you, boy—' he hoisted Bill on to his bunk. 'Get under the covers there and be quiet . . . '

When they had each drunk deeply from cups of steaming tea, Joe, holding the bedclothes up under his chin with one hand, asked, 'What do you make of it, Jonathan?'

Jonathan did not answer immediately, and when he did it was to the point. 'She couldn't have moved off on her own,' he said.

'Them on *The Night Star*,' said Joe. 'They were on to us. The mistake we made was not keepin' awake.'

45

'I hate to think that they would do it,' said Malcolm. 'I feel the man Sloper would, but not the owner. I still think he's a nice man.'

'Look,' said Joe. 'He's bound to know what's going on on his own boat, isn't he?'

'If he was there,' answered Malcolm. 'You didn't see him, did you, Jonathan?'

'No. No, I didn't see him,' said Jonathan; 'or hear him. I would have recognized his voice; it's different from the rest.'

'Well,' said Joe, 'we can easily find out if he's aboard. As soon as it's daylight let's go back and see if he's on the boat. We'll have to go back in any case for the anchors . . . that's if they haven't swiped them.'

'What time is it?' asked Malcolm now.

'Half past two,' said Jonathan, looking at his watch hanging from the book rack.

'How long do you think we were adrift?' asked Joe.

'No idea, not the faintest. But I know this. If it hadn't been for him—' Jonathan put out his hand and fondled Bill's head, the only part of him visible from under the covers '—goodness knows what might have happened.'

'You're right there,' said Joe, jerking his thumb towards Bill. 'Good old Bill. But there's another thing.' He looked at Jonathan again. 'Why didn't he bark when he heard them at the ropes, eh?'

'That's a question,' said Jonathan.

'It only goes to prove,' said Joe, 'that whoever loosened them was an expert at doing things on the quiet, for his nibs usually barks at the slightest strange noise, now doesn't he?'

Jonathan made no answer to this but his brows gathered thoughtfully.

'Would the boat have turned over, do you think?' Malcolm now asked with a slight note of apprehension in his voice.

'No, I don't think so,' said Jonathan. 'But she could have gone headlong into the river bank at some place where there are obstructions, such as piles sticking up, and had her bottom ripped . . . Oh well,' he sighed; 'it's no use sitting up here until daylight; we can't puzzle it out any further at present, so we might as well try to get some sleep for an hour or so, then we'll go back as soon as it's light and take it from there.'

'Yes; and take it from there,' endorsed Joe firmly.

They talked spasmodically for a while longer; then again all was quiet in *The Mary Ann Shaughnessy*.

3

But they didn't go back to Burwell Lode at first light. It was just on eight o'clock when Jonathan woke up. Looking at his watch, he couldn't believe what it told him and so, reaching up to the sideboard, he switched on the radio, and the sound awoke the others.

'Coo!' said Joe, turning his head into his pillow. 'What time is it?'

'Nearly eight by my watch, if it's right.'

The voice of the announcer filled the cabin now, saying, 'A plane crashed while taking off from Rome last evening. There were no survivors of the thirty-six passengers aboard, three of whom were British ... No trace has yet been found of the lorry driver, Edward Williams, but his lorry was found abandoned in a wood outside Windsor ... Thieves got away with jewellery to the value of fifty thousand pounds from Green Glades, the home of Mr Charles Walmer, on the River Thames ...'

'Oh, switch that off,' muttered Malcolm now under his breath; 'I've got a beastly head.'

As Jonathan switched off the radio Joe exclaimed loudly, 'Aw, man, it could have been something. Didn't you hear about jewels being stolen? It could have been them.'

'Don't talk rot, Joe,' said Jonathan impatiently. 'How could it have been the crew of *The Night Star* stealing from somewhere on the River Thames when here we are thinking that they pushed us off last night? They couldn't be in two places at once.'

'But he didn't say the jewels were pinched last night,' said Joe.

'Well, use your loaf. They don't usually give two days old news, do they? And look,' Jonathan wagged his finger down at Joe. 'Don't start imagining things along those lines, else it's going to get us into trouble.'

'But, Jonathan.' It was Malcolm speaking now, and very quietly. 'What about last night? I mean the van, and the man you saw in the back of it.'

In the act of pulling on his sweater, Jonathan paused; then, his head slowly emerging through the roll-topped neck, he looked down on Malcolm before dropping on to the end of the bunk again and saying slowly, 'Yes; yes, you have something, but . . . but didn't the announcer say the lorry was found in Windsor?'

'Something like that,' said Joe, kneeling up on the bunk now, his small body quivering with excitement. 'But these gangs have got fast cars, and helicopters, and—' he stabbed his finger down towards Malcolm's nose '—boats like *The Night Star.*'

'Oh! Oh!' Jonathan was on his feet again, his head wagging. 'There you go, taking it too far, as usual.'

49

'All right, but let's wait an' see, eh?' said Joe. 'And when we get back we can have a look round. We can be taking Bill for a walk, and we could admire *The Night Star*, couldn't we? There's no law against that. We could even act dim and say we were blown off the bank in the night with the high wind.'

'We'll see when we get there,' said Jonathan, starting up the engine. 'And while we are going, you can both put the bedding away and tidy up generally, and we'll have breakfast in the creek.'

It was a good half-an-hour later when *The Mary Ann Shaughnessy* turned into Burwell Lode again because Jonathan had gone down river for some distance before realizing he was heading the wrong way and so had to turn round again and make his way back. They were all looking ahead expectantly as they rounded a slight bend in the river where it neared the Lode, but there was no white *Night Star* moored against the bank.

'She might be round the corner in our place,' whispered Malcolm.

A minute later they steered into the creek, and there on the bank they saw their rond anchors, still stuck well into the ground. But there was no sign of *The Night Star*.

As they tied the ropes once more to the anchors Joe said, 'As you were sayin', Jonathan, the wind was high, but it wouldn't unloosen two of the ropes at once, man. An' you tied one yourself. I could imagine mine coming undone but not your two half-hitches.'

Jonathan said nothing to this for he was per-
plexed, and not a little worried, but the latter
feeling he kept to himself.

After they'd had breakfast they washed *The
Mary Ann* down, polished her brass, cleaned the
cabin and galley, then swam in the river to cool
off, whilst Bill barked his lungs out from the
bank.

Then came the business of getting dinner ready,
which made Joe remark that it was nothing but
bloomin' cleaning, cooking, and washing-up . . .

They set out again, but did not see a sign of
habitation until they caught sight of the majestic
Ely Cathedral on the skyline and they hailed it
like men who hadn't seen land for weeks.

As they turned at The Fish and Duck Inn into
the old West River, Malcolm said, 'Have you
thought, Jonathan, that if we continue up here
we'll have to go through a number of locks?' He
lifted his head from the map. 'This river, the old
West, is a great length, ten or eleven miles long
I think. The first lock is Hermitage; then there's
Brownshill lock, and St Ives; and, oh Lord, dozens
of others after that.'

'Coo!' There came a long drawn-out groan from
Joe. 'Just let your imagination roam an' see
us goin' through them with his nibs here.' He
thumbed towards Bill who was lying at peace
now on top of the locker.

'All right, you've made your point,' said Jonathan, trying not to laugh. Then looking at
Malcolm again, he asked, 'Are there any locks
the other way?'

51

After a moment Malcolm replied, 'No. If we were to go back into the main river and up to Ely it looks as if we could travel miles and not see the sight of one, except at Denver Sluice, and that looks a big daddy of a lock.' He turned and looked at Bill affectionately now, saying, 'You'd like this one, boy; it looks as if it could swallow the *Queen Elizabeth*.' Then turning to the map again he said, 'There's lots of rivers going off the main one; the Wissey, the Brandon, the Lark . . . '

'Oh, there looks as if there's a lock right up the Lark,' said Jonathan. 'But Uncle Tom didn't think much of the Lark. I remember him saying it was very shallow at the top end and *The Mary Ann*'s draught was too deep for it.'

'Well, shipmates!' exclaimed Malcolm, straightening up. 'There's a phone by the second bridge along here, and after we've phoned home we can come back and do the lot of them. And *no locks!*' He had been accompanied in the last three words by Joe, and they shook hands solemnly, then punched at each other and laughed.

Now Joe, a spasm of excitement passing through him, jumped up on to the foredeck and, throwing out his hands, cried, 'Look! No locks.' Then taking his antics further, he went on in a loud voice, 'Ladies an' gentlemen. During the conducted tour on *The Mary Ann Shaughnessy*, I will bring to your notice points of interest. On your right . . . sorry starboard, we are passing eight cows. No sir, I am wrong again. Ten cows. Please to note their black-and-white faces. On the port side we are approaching what looks like the old dark house. Note it well, ladies an' gentlemen.'

52

Jonathan and Malcolm were both laughing heartily now, and Jonathan shouted up at Joe, 'And for your interest, ladies and gentlemen, our guide is slightly misinformed, for the cows happen to be heifers.'

'Well, ladies an' gentlemen,' Joe began again, 'whatever the captain says . . . ' He stopped abruptly and stood pointing ahead to where a huge grey bird, lifting itself slowly from the bank, flew across their path, its long legs hanging like ropes beneath it.

'Oh!' Jonathan leant over the side of the boat, without leaving go of the wheel, and cried excitedly, 'It's a heron! It's a heron! And look, there's another.' The herons flew away along the river bank. Then as the boat approached them again, they flew over the fenland and into the great expanse of sky.

'What do you bet we won't see a crocodile sliding into the great waters ahead of us?' said Joe from the deck, demonstrating with a wide wave of his hand. 'And on the next bend but one there'll be a herd of elephants, you'll see.'

'There's a boat coming.' Malcolm was standing on the locker, his head through the hatchway, and now whispering excitedly, he added, 'I've an idea it's *The Night Star*.'

Jonathan stood up quickly and Joe, stopping his fooling, dropped down into the cockpit, and they all waited as they rounded the bend, and sure enough the boat coming towards them was *The Night Star*.

The old West River was narrow for most of its length, except where it swelled into a largish

53

bay below The Royal Oak Inn, but the stretch along which *The Mary Ann* was now chugging was very narrow indeed and Jonathan had to ᵗake her well to starboard and into a mass of water lilies. *The Night Star*, as she should have been, was moving over to her right side of the river, but she was not slowing down and the deep wash this caused pushed *The Mary Ann* through the water lilies and well into the bank; and there she stuck. As *The Night Star* towered above them the boys, all glaring at Sloper at the wheel, protested loudly, and Jonathan, on this occasion, loudest of all. 'Can't you go a little slower! You're the one who makes a mighty fuss about people bumping you.'

The Night Star well past now, Sloper turned and shouted from the wheelhouse, 'Go and fry your face.'

'And you go and get your ugly face lifted,' yelled Joe, and for once Jonathan did not chastise him.

When eventually *The Mary Ann*'s bows were released from the mud they continued their journey, talking all the while indignantly about *The Night Star* and her crew, and as they entered the bay at The Royal Oak, Malcolm ended the discussion by saying, 'But don't forget we didn't see the owner; I'd like to bet you tuppence he wasn't aboard.'

As soon as they had berthed at the end of the bay they made their way towards the inn that lay above the river bank. They had to watch their step for the bank was strewn with tents, the guy ropes almost coming to the water's edge. The tents seemingly were housing complete families, including dogs, and on Bill's approach they set up a loud protest, but it was Bill's one virtue that he never barked or stepped out of line when on the lead. Should he growl under his breath to show his displeasure he knew he would soon be checked by a tug on his collar, and since he was one who rarely wasted energy on something that had no end in view he appeared the most docile of dogs when attended by one or other of the boys.

When they reached the back door of the inn they were met by the lady of the house. 'Yes?' she said. 'You want water?'

'No, thank you,' said Jonathan. 'Our name's Crawford. We're on *The Mary Ann Shaughnessy*. My uncle, Mr Cookson, said you would allow us to phone from here and have mail left.'

'Oh!' exclaimed Mrs Burgess. 'Come in, come in.' She stood aside and they followed each other into the little kitchen, Malcolm bringing up the rear with Bill.

Bill had his nose to the ground and an unusual sensation was prickling his spine; it wasn't aggressive, nor was it the joyful feeling that he experienced when meeting up with a lady dog. The feeling was engendered by the smell of a black poodle sitting at the far side of the hearth.

'Now, Dandy,' said Mrs Burgess, 'behave . . . Is he all right?' She looked at Bill, and by way of answer Malcolm asked, 'Is she a bitch?'

'I'm afraid not; but he's very good with other dogs.'

'I wish we could say that of ours,' said Malcolm ruefully. Then he had almost to chew back the

55

inference because Bill's tail, from a small movement, began to wag vigorously and, his bandy legs buckling under him, he lowered himself on to the floor and there awaited the black poodle's approach. And when they shook hands with their noses the boys laughed, and, looking at Mrs Burgess, they exclaimed, one after the other, words to the effect of, 'What do you think of that!'

'You want to use the phone? Then go ahead; it's just in the passage,' said Mrs Burgess.

While Jonathan phoned through to home, Mrs Burgess handed Malcolm and Joe each a hot pasty, so hot that Malcolm had to release his hold on Bill's lead. Within a second, realizing what he had done, he made a grab at the strap, only to see it lying limply on the floor, and Bill lying as limply beside it, while he stared entranced at the black poodle. 'Look!' He nudged Joe. 'Would you believe it!'

'No, I don't,' said Joe. 'Although I'm seein' it I'm not believin' it.'

It was at this moment that a tap came on the door and a polite voice said, 'Good afternoon. My name is Leech; I'm the owner of *The Night Star*. Can you tell me if she has been in the bay?'

As Mrs Burgess moved towards the door the boys gasped at the man standing there.

'*The Night Star*?' said Mrs Burgess, pausing a moment. 'No; nor have I seen her, but she might have passed down unknown to me.'

'Yes, yes, she did.' Malcolm moved to Mrs Burgess's side and, looking up at Mr Leech added, 'She passed us about half-an-hour ago and she pushed . . . ' He stopped.

56

'Why, hello!' Mr Leech beamed down, first on Malcolm, and then on Joe. 'You're the boys from the *Miss Shaughnessy*, aren't you?'

'*The Mary Ann Shaughnessy*,' corrected Malcolm.

'Oh, *The Mary Ann Shaughnessy*.' Mr Leech moved his head in deep nods and glanced at Mrs Burgess as he repeated, 'I mustn't forget her full title; that would never do.' Then, looking at Malcolm again, he asked, 'Well, how are you enjoying it?'

'Oh, very well, sir . . . '

' . . . Except that in the night somebody untied our ropes and set us adrift.' Joe was staring up into Mr Leech's face, and Mr Leech, shaking his head gravely, said, 'No! Really? That's a dirty trick. Had you been getting on the wrong side of the village boys, because they are known to retaliate, you know?'

'I don't think it was the village boys. Anyway, we hadn't seen anybody except . . . '

'Good afternoon, sir,' Jonathan said from the doorway, cutting off Joe's words.

'Oh . . . good afternoon,' said Mr Leech. Then after a short pause he added, 'The boys tell me you were adrift in the night, but none of you look any the worse for the adventure. These things happen on big and little boats alike and, as I say, you learn a lot when you're in charge of a boat.'

'Yes, you do, sir.' Jonathan's expression was unusually straight.

'Well, I must away and find mine now. I'll likely pick her up at Ely. I slipped up to London last night to see a friend and did not stipulate at

57

what time I would be back.' He was addressing Mrs Burgess now, and she, nodding at him, replied, 'Well, she can't be far. Somebody will have seen her; there's a jungle telegraph keeps tabs on the movement of boats on the river.'

Mr Leech smiled; then looking at the boys he said, 'It's more than possible we'll run into each other again . . . but not in the lock I hope.' Giving a low chuckle, he walked to a big black car parked at the side of the inn, and a moment later he was driving away down the main road.

'Well, what did I tell you?' said Malcolm now. 'He wasn't on board. He's a nice man. I knew he was.'

Jonathan made no answer to this but, turning to Mrs Burgess, said gravely, 'There may be a letter coming. I gave them this address; is that all right?'

'Of course, of course,' said Mrs Burgess.

'Thank you very much. Goodbye.'

Joe and Malcolm, too, added their goodbyes. Then out on the lawn near the little garden pool they stood looking at Jonathan, and it was Malcolm who asked, 'What is it? What's happened?'

'The postman's taken the case up. Father's got to appear a week tomorrow, so we must get Bill back by then.'

'NO!'

'Oh, that's bad,' said Joe.

'But he just broke a little bit of skin on his calf!' cried Malcolm, his face all twisted up now. 'He never bites people, only dogs. Everybody knows that. The postman knows that, and if he hadn't picked the golf club up off the lawn and swung it Bill would never have gone for him. He wasn't to know he was just playing; he thought he was coming at him . . . We explained.'

'Well, apparently he didn't take our explanation. This is the second time it's happened.'

'Well, he didn't even break the skin the other time.'

'He's a bull terrier,' said Jonathan, now looking down at Bill, 'and people are frightened of bull terriers. They know that once they get a grip they won't let go.'

'But they must realize that he had no intention of biting the postman,' Malcolm went on protesting. 'If he had he could have taken all the flesh off his calf. But what did he do? Broke the skin . . . just a tiny bit of skin.'

'His leg was all bruised. Don't forget that.'

'*Bruised!*' Malcolm exclaimed scornfully, turning his back on the other two. 'This has put the damper on everything. How can we be expected to enjoy the holiday with that sentence hanging over him?' Then turning back to Jonathan, he said angrily, 'I won't let them put him to sleep. I won't! I *won't!*'

'Be quiet. Keep your voice down. People are looking at you.' And now Jonathan turned to Joe, and very quietly he said, 'and there's a message for you, Joe.' He paused a moment as he looked into Joe's straight face. 'Your mother called to see you yesterday.'

On this Malcolm, too, turned and looked at Joe. He saw his eyes seeming to get larger while his face became thinner, almost pinched-looking.

Joe had to gather some saliva into his mouth before he could ask, 'Did she leave a message?'

'She's written you a letter,' said Jonathan softly. 'She wrote it in our house. Mother gave her this address, so you should get it tomorrow.'

Jonathan and Malcolm, standing now close together, watched Joe turn away and walk down the bank towards the river, and they did not attempt to follow him.

'He's upset at missing her,' said Malcolm. 'I wonder why she came back? Do you think she's going to stay?'

'I shouldn't imagine it from what mother says. I think she's going to get a divorce.'

'No . . ! Oh good Lord! Poor Joe. Although he doesn't say much he's been hoping all the time that she'd get lonely and come back . . . He's . . . he's lonely, Jonathan.'

'I know,' said Jonathan. 'And he'll be more so if they get a divorce; that'll be final then.'

They were just about to move forward towards the steps that led down to the river bank when there came to them the sound of yelling and shouting. It was the kind of commotion that they recognized, and immediately both of them looked round about them, but Bill was no longer there. Like two rockets, they made for the steps and there, standing poised for a moment, they surveyed the scene below them: cursing men, yelling women, screaming children, frantic barking dogs and all going round in circles, and in the middle of them a tent that was leaning well to leeward.

Malcolm, bounding down the steps behind Jonathan, yelled with him, 'Bill! Bill! Here boy.

Here boy.' But their combined cries were lost in the hullaballoo into which they dived.

'Catch the devil.'

'He's eaten the lot . . . Look at the tent!'

'Mind the baby! Mind the baby!'

'All my gentles in the river! I'll brain him when I get him.'

'Go for him, Rover! Go for him. Worry him. Go on, Rover, worry him!'

It is doubtful if Bill had ever been in such a commotion in his eventful life. He knew what it was to be harassed, chased, beaten on the nose, approached with a stick, and even kicked, but never the lot at once like this, and he considered it so very unfair. Moreover, he was in no fighting mood. All he had done was to follow the black poodle down the steps and along the river bank, experiencing the strange feeling, a sort of pallyness which was definitely new to him for up till now he had either loved or hated; then into this calm new world there had been wafted to him a delightful aroma, and he had been amazed to find the source within sniffing distance of his nose. When he took his eyes from Dandy's rump, there it was, a whole furry rabbit, all ready for catching, and without any impediment. He had reasoned that if it wasn't meant for him it would have been out of reach, and so, diverging from the path behind Dandy, he just quietly picked up the rabbit . . . And that's when the quietness ended.

The scare the woman gave him coming behind him like that had shot him into the tent where he came into collision with a number of strange objects, not least a small child who not only screamed at him but grabbed at the rabbit. Now everybody was going mad at once, and all putting obstacles in his way, such as tins full of worms, fishing lines, cans, water jugs, mattresses, primus stoves and frying pans, and when one of the latter, hurling through the air, hit him on the rump he gave a deep yelp and bounded yet once again, this time almost landing in the river which he did his best to prevent for he didn't care overmuch for water when seen from dry land, and he abhorred what was known as swimming in it. His front paws in the water, his hind paws gripping at the sloping bank, he hung suspended while the comforting voice of Joe yelled above him, 'You kick him if you dare!'

'I'll kick you in an' all. If I'd a gun I'd shoot him. Look at this place. Look what he's done.'

'It wasn't his fault; he didn't start it.'

'We'll report you. We'll summons you.' There were several threatening faces around Joe when Jonathan pushed forward and helped Joe to pull Bill up the bank. Then holding Bill's collar, he said, 'He's my dog; I'm responsible. But he's done no harm to anyone. He didn't bite, or anything.'

'Well for you he didn't. But look at this place. Did you ever see anything like it?'

'We'll help you to get it straight.'

'I don't want your help, I want this damage made good,' said a man in a blue jersey.

'Oh, hold your hand a moment.' They all turned to look at a man stepping out of a boat called *The Fen Fire*. He was holding his jaw with one hand and gripping his waist with the other, as was the

62

woman who was sitting in the well of the boat; in fact, she was doubled up with painful laughter. 'As the boy says,' gasped the man, 'the dog's done no real harm. I saw all that happened. He was walking quietly along and there, level with his nose, was a rabbit lying on a fishing stool. What do you expect a dog to do? Walk past? If your wife hadn't scared him there would have been none of this.'

'Go on, blame it on my wife.'

'I'm not blaming it on anyone,' said the tall man. 'I'm only going to say it's the funniest thing I've seen in my life; I only wish I'd had a camera.'

A restless lull settled on the group of campers. Then one of the women made a little sound in her throat, and, looking at the man in the blue jersey, she said softly, 'He's right you know, it was funny. Even when I was running round like mad trying to catch our Rover, and you were yelling at him to worry the bull terrier—' she nodded at Bill '—I kept thinking, I know who'll be worried if they meet up, and it struck me it was like a comic movie.'

'Aye, it's all very well, but . . . ' The man's voice trailed away as a number of sniggers developed into laughter, in which he made a successful effort not to join. Instead, still unbending, he nodded at Jonathan, saying, 'Well, get it away before it decides to eat the baby.'

'Oh, Stan!' The woman who had caused the rumpus pushed at her husband and remarked, 'It's a funny thing, but I nearly had a fit when I saw the baby grab at the rabbit in his mouth, and I couldn't believe my eyes when he let it go.

You know our Rover wouldn't do that; he growls at the baby if she comes near him when he's got a bone.'

'You'll be pinning a medal on the ugly brute next,' said the man, glaring at Bill. Then looking at the boys, he added, 'Go on, get off, the lot of you.' He waved them away, but they needed no second bidding.

No-one spoke until they were on the boat, when Jonathan said flatly, 'There's nothing for it, we'll have to find some place quiet and stay there. We'll just have to keep away from the villages and the towns.'

There was silence in the cockpit for a moment. Then Joe, dropping his head back on to his shoulders, and his eyes ranging over the great expanse of open sky, said, 'It's going to be a smashing trip. We mustn't go through locks, we mustn't go into towns and villages and we must cut the holiday short to get him back for his sentence. Oh yes, it's going to be a real smasher, full of beef and adventure.'

Both Jonathan and Malcolm looked at Joe, but they did not make a retort suitable to his scathing statement, because each knew that he was not really thinking about the trip at all. He was not even thinking of Bill's fate, because he was, at this moment, very upset that he had not been at home when his mother came to see him.

4

Later that day they proceeded down the old West and into the main river, made a short stop at Ely where they did some shopping, then went on past the beet factory, along the blank, seemingly never-ending straight stretch to Littleport, after which they carried on along the Ten Mile Bank, and to The Ship Inn.

The inn was situated at the point where the Little Ouse, or Brandon Creek as it was usually known, flowed into the main river, and they berthed a short distance up the creek.

The following morning they went on up the Brandon, to discover it was a comparatively wide river, until they came to the Cross-Water staunch. This afforded them some excitement and helped to dispel the remnants of yesterday's tension, because they had to fight their way through it. The staunch was blocked with massive clumps of river reeds that had been cut by the reed cutter into miniature islands to be taken away by the 'stream' but had become lodged in the narrow channel.

After several fruitless efforts to get through they welcomed the advice from the man at the pumphouse who shouted to them, 'Go in full steam ahead, then shut her off and she'll glide through.' And she did glide through.

All the way up the river to Wilton Bridge the boys encountered these large floating islands of reeds, and if Joe had had his way they would have gone head on through each pile instead of avoiding them.

It was late evening of the same day when, after coming down the river again, they found a clear space for berthing on the left bank some two hundred yards below an empty house that stood on the other side of the river. The house windows were boarded, and its lower half was lost in a tangle of overgrown brambles and weeds. The place intrigued the boys and they decided that the following morning they would take the boat across to the other side and find a place to moor, then have a look round the house.

It wasn't the first empty house they had seen on the banks. These houses were disused public houses that had once served the barge men when the river was a thriving source of transport, but were now too far off the beaten track and too lacking in amenities to be habitable.

The sun had been shining all that day and had helped to lighten their somewhat depressed spirits, and when Malcolm suggested that they should have a swim before their evening meal Jonathan voted it a good idea. But Joe declined, saying he didn't feel like a swim; he felt a bit shivery.

Jonathan's sympathy seemed mixed when he advised him to take a couple of aspirins and make a start on preparing the meal, and a few minutes later he and Malcolm dropped over the side into the water to the accompaniment of Bill's barking. Their destination was the reed cutter, which they had passed earlier in the day at work further up the river. It was now lying down river, together with a long iron barge, and when they came abreast of it they couldn't get near it because of the cut reeds floating on the surface of the water. So, instead of resting by hanging on to the side of the barge, they turned and swam back to the boat.

It had been a longish swim and they were very tired when they climbed aboard, and Jonathan grumbled a bit at the slow progress Joe had made towards providing them with something to eat.

When eventually they had eaten and reluctantly washed up they did not have a game of cards as they had done on the previous night, but they all turned in, and when the light was out they lay quiet, each taken up with his own thoughts, Jonathan and Malcolm wondering what was to be Bill's fate in seven days' time, and Joe, his face buried in his pillow, thinking about his mother.

Bill had been asleep for some time; he, too, was very tired. Having been stung on his hind quarters by a wasp as he sat on the bank early that morning, following which he had broken all his previous records as he raced in a series of wide circles, he had spent most of the day licking his extremity and longing in his doggy mind for the peace and security of home, until at last he had found forgetfulness in sleep. So, for once he wasn't alert to the approaching footsteps, but when he heard the thumping on the roof and a voice yelling 'Hi! You in there!' he sprang off the bunk, barking furiously while dashing the short distance from one door to the other.

'Stop it! Hold on!'

'Who's that?'

'What is it?'

'What's the matter?'

'What's happened?'

They were all talking at once when the voice from outside called again, 'It's the police. Come out here a minute.'

'Police!' Jonathan switched on the light and the boys squinted at each other; then, scrambling out of their bunks, they pulled open the door and tumbled into the cockpit, and after Jonathan had unloosened the awning by the side of the hatch they all stood blinking furiously as they turned their sleep-filled eyes from the light of the torch.

'Well now, what have you been up to?'

'I don't know what you mean. What's the matter?' said Jonathan.

'Haven't you got ears, or have you got used to the sound?'

'Ears?' Malcolm and Joe looked at each other.

'Well, listen a minute.'

So they all listened. And then they heard it, a deep *chunk! chunk! chunk!* of a machine at work.

'Somebody's set the reed cutter going.'

'Well, I can assure you it wasn't us,' said Jonathan indignantly.

'No?' said the police officer. 'Well, that's for you to prove. But you swam up to it a short while ago, didn't you?'

'Yes. Yes, we did.'

'And you didn't get on board?'

'No; we couldn't because of the reeds in the river.'

'That's a thin excuse. Get your clothes on.'

'What!'

'I said you'd better get your clothes on, the lot of you.'

They squinted up into the light again; then, turning in a bemused fashion, they went into the cabin and struggled into their clothes.

'Stay there,' said Jonathan, pushing Bill's muzzle away as he shut him in the cabin, and, taking no notice of his howling and barking, he stepped on to the bank and joined Malcolm, Joe and the policeman.

'Now we'll go along the bank and across the river in the chain ferry and you'll get in there and stop that machine. But that won't be the end of it . . . Come on.'

'Look here.' Jonathan stood his ground. 'We can't do that, for the simple reason we never set her going. I know nothing about the reed cutter, none of us do. You're barking up the wrong tree.'

'Never mind about barking up wrong trees, you come along.'

'Who said it was us?' asked Joe now.

'Well, since you ask, we had a phone call. You were seen swimming down the river and boarding her.'

'It's a downright lie.'

'Come on,' said the policeman tersely, ignoring Jonathan's denial. And such was his manner that they came on, stumbling in the wavering torchlight along the rough bank until they came to an old black punt.

Bewildered, they boarded her, and the policeman, pulling on the chain, drew them slowly to the other side. Then after stumbling on again they came to the reed cutter, with its knives thrashing at the water, and, standing looking down at it, was another policeman. Turning, he said, 'Well, you got them.'

'They say they know nothing about it.'

'Oh, no?' The second policeman looked at Jonathan. 'You still at school?'

'Yes,' said Jonathan.

'Well, tell me by way of interest what you intend to be when you leave.'

Jonathan, looking from one man to the other through the beam of light, said after a moment, 'An engineer, I hope.'

'Well, that's better than a burglar, and it explains your knowledge of machinery. But still I'd like to know how you picked the lock.'

'*Me!* Pick a lock . . ? You're mad.'

'Now, now!' The other policeman's voice was sharp.

'Well, you are, both of you. I tell you flatly we don't know a thing about it.'

'You've admitted swimming down to here.'

'Yes. Yes. But I told you we couldn't get near because of the reeds. Look, switch your light on to the river. Go on.'

When the policeman's powerful torch flashed over the water, it revealed a wide expanse of floating reed, except around the immediate cutters where the water was clear.

The policemen looked at each other; then the first one said, 'I see what he means, but—' turning to Jonathan he ended, 'that doesn't say you couldn't have come up the bank and got into her.'

'How would I have picked the lock without some tool or other? I was swimming, remember.'

'There's plenty of bits of wire and odd things lying round on her,' said the second policeman.

Jonathan ignored this statement and his silence told Malcolm that he was very angry, so in a quiet voice Malcolm made a suggestion to the policeman. 'You could break the glass in the cabin window and get in her that way,' he said.

'We're not breaking any glass, young man, if we can help it.'

The two policemen now moved away along the bank and their whispering was inaudible to the boys. Then the first man, coming back, said, 'Well, if you can't help us you can't. But I'd better have your names and know where you're off to tomorrow as I may want to talk to you again. This is a serious offence, you know.'

'Well, we didn't commit the offence,' said Jonathan bitterly. 'And whoever phoned you had more knowledge of it than any of us . . . Who was it phoned you, anyway?'

'We don't know that, we just got word from the station that some boys from a boat up the river had been tampering with the reed cutter and set it going.'

'Well, if you got the person who phoned you'd likely get the one who did the job,' put in Joe; and to this neither of the policemen made any comment, but the second man said, 'I'd better go into Ely and see if I can contact Bert Wilson and bring him out, while you get them across the river again.'

A short time later, when the policeman was about to leave them at the boat, he said, 'You didn't say where you're off to tomorrow.'

'We don't rightly know yet. Perhaps to Denver Sluice, and then up the River Wissey.'

'Ah well, there's plenty of roads round that quarter, not like here. We'll be able to pick you up if we want you. I'd advise you to stay around there. Now you'd better get back into bed, the lot of you.'

'Thank you for nothing,' muttered Joe as he entered the cabin. 'Pick you up!' he mimicked. 'Makes you feel like a criminal. Stop it, man! Stop it!' he pushed at Bill as he bounded from one to the other.

'Lie down!' said Jonathan as he hauled Bill up on to the bunk. Then sitting down beside him he looked at the other two, now sitting opposite, and said simply, 'Well?'

'It's fishy,' said Joe. 'That's what it is, fishy. Somebody's trying to pin something on us. First sending us adrift, and now this. They want to make things so hot that we'll give up the trip. That's how I see it.'

And for a moment Jonathan, too, saw it that way, but his cautious nature made him say, 'Don't go off on that tack again. It's likely one of the village fellows, as that Mr Leech said; perhaps he saw us swimming and thought it would be a lark.'

'Yes, that could be,' said Malcolm, looking at Joe. 'I remember Uncle Tom saying a lot of the

boys had their own territories for swimming and
that they didn't like anybody else butting in. And
after all, we are butting in, I mean we people
on the boats.'

There was another short silence; then Joe said
suddenly, 'About tomorrow. You said we were
going up to Denver Sluice and that way . . . What
about my letter? I thought we were going back to
The Royal Oak where I could pick it up.'

'I'd forgotten about that,' said Jonathan softly
now. 'But he told us to stay up this end, and we'll
have to unless we want more trouble. But I tell
you what. You could get off at The Ship Inn and
walk up to the main road where there's a bus
that will take you near there. How about that?'

'Yes . . . Yes, I could do that.' Joe nodded.

'Well, then,' said Jonathan, yawning, 'that's
settled. So, come on, let's try again. We've had
one night's rest in three, and I for one am begin-
ning to feel it. It seems that there's a jinx on us
or something.'

He was sorry the moment he had said it. It was
enough to have one of that turn of mind aboard.
He glanced at Joe and said, on a laugh now,
'Bring us back some of those Cornish pasties Mrs
Burgess does. Run all the way back with them so
they'll still be hot.'

'I'll charter a plane,' said Joe.

The following morning Joe left *The Mary Ann
Shaughnessy* to go to The Royal Oak to pick up
his letter, and he never returned.

5

Jonathan had dropped Joe off at the bottom of the Brandon and had made arrangements with him to pick him up again at some point opposite the entrance to the River Wissey. He reckoned that Joe should be back around dinner time, depending on the buses and how they ran. They would then explore the Wissey up past Hilgay and the sugar beet factory where, he understood, there were some wide lakes which originally had been quarries and, what was more to the point with a view to curtailing Bill's antics, not often frequented.

At one o'clock *The Mary Ann Shaughnessy* was tied up in the main river opposite where the Wissey branched off. Jonathan had berthed her here because there was a roadway just over the bank and they could keep a look-out for the bus because, unless Joe was sitting on the upper deck, he would be unable to see the boat in the river.

When two o'clock came Malcolm said for the third time, 'Well, I tell you, Jonathan, it wasn't clear how you explained it. You said something about we might go up to Denver Sluice, and you know he was so taken up with getting his letter I bet he didn't take in half of what you were saying . . . Look, let's go up to Denver.'

At half-past two Jonathan had made for Denver. Since they had first set out from Cambridge he had looked forward to seeing this great engineering feat. He had read all about Labely, the Swiss, who had constructed the miracle of engineering after the previous dam had collapsed in 1713, but all his reading hadn't conveyed the awesome sight of the sluice, compared with which *The Mary Ann Shaughnessy* was like a floating leaf on the water. He would have liked nothing better than to have spent the rest of the day just looking at the dam, but after standing gazing down into the great well for some minutes in blank silence, Malcolm had urged, 'Come on, Bill's getting nervous. Look at him, he's all bristles; he thinks we're going through.'

'Well, we wouldn't be much use without the boat, would we?' Jonathan gave a weak smile, then added, 'Oh, I'd like to spend a day here.'

'Well, we can always come back when we've picked up Joe. Come on.'

Jonathan turned and walked away, knowing that it wasn't only Bill who was nervous of this great towering pile of iron and stone, but that Malcolm, too, didn't like it.

After again going up river and berthing opposite the Wissey, they stood for a time in the roadway, watching and waiting; then they went along to a house and asked if anyone had seen a boy waiting about. But no; no-one had seen a boy of any sort.

On board again, they headed up the Wissey, oblivious now of the colourful banks where grew tall reeds, purple loosestrife and willowherb in profusion. And so they came to Hilgay, where a crowd of boys and girls were swimming in the river, some of them seeming to be standing up almost in the middle of it.

'It looks like the local swimming pool,' remarked Malcolm, and Jonathan answered tersely, 'Well, local or otherwise, we won't use it . . . look over there.' He nodded to the side, to where three dogs were gambolling playfully together. 'His nibs would soon break that up,' he ended flatly.

Five minutes later Jonathan walked along the bank to where the children were swimming, and he called to them, 'Have you noticed a boy round here—' he lifted his hand to simulate Joe's height '—black hair, thin, waiting about?'

The children called to each other now; 'Anyone seen a boy waitin' around, on the bridge or anywhere?'

No; no-one had seen a stranger . . .

It was five o'clock when Jonathan went to the phone, leaving Malcolm on board with Bill. When he got through to The Royal Oak Mrs Burgess answered him brightly. Oh, yes, the young lad had called just after ten this morning. And yes, there had been a letter for him. Was there anything wrong?

Jonathan explained to her that Joe hadn't returned and she answered, 'Oh well now, I would see to that because he's had time to get to London and back, hasn't he? Come to think of it, he looked a little depressed after he read his letter,

76

and I gave him a bag of crisps and a pasty. But he didn't eat them I noticed, just stuffed them in his pocket . . . It's very worrying this. Now listen, if he doesn't turn up within the next hour or so you'll have to do something.'

'Yes, yes, I will,' Jonathan answered. 'Thank you.'

When he returned to the boat he gazed at Malcolm for a moment before saying, 'He got there, and got his letter. Mrs Burgess said he was depressed after he read it . . . What do you think?'

'I know.' Malcolm nodded slowly now. 'I'd like to bet he's gone home. I bet you a shilling, Jonathan, he's gone home. Don't you think you'd better phone and ask? . . . Is the phone very far away?'

'The other end of the village, but that doesn't matter. I'll do that. Yes, I'll do that.'

Again Jonathan was hurrying through the village, and when he got in touch with his home it was his father who answered the phone.

'Oh, hello there, boy,' he called, in his breezy fashion. 'Nice to hear you. How's things going?'

'Father,' said Jonathan immediately, 'has Joe come home?'

'Joe? Come home? Why should he?'

'Well. Well, he went to The Royal Oak this morning and picked up a letter from his mother. This was around ten, and he hasn't come back. Mrs Burgess said he seemed depressed so we thought he might have made for home.'

'Good gracious! Look, hang on a minute; I'll slip next door and make sure. Yet if he had come home he would surely have been in here.'

In the meantime, Jonathan had to keep supplying the phone with coins. Then Mr Crawford's voice came again: it was grave-sounding now as he said, 'No, he's not there.'

'What do you think I should do, Father?'

'How long do you say he's been away?'

'He got off the boat at nine o'clock this morning.'

'Are you sure you got your meeting places right?'

'Yes, yes, I'm positive. But Malcolm thought that he might have got mixed up, so we've been to the places I mentioned to him before he left, Denver Sluice and Hilgay. We're at Hilgay now.'

'Well now, listen to me. What you must do right away is to go to the village police and explain the situation to them.'

'But what if he turns up, we'll look silly.'

'It doesn't matter about looking silly, boy.' Mr Crawford was shouting. 'You'll look sillier if you wait until tomorrow and he doesn't turn up.'

'Yes. All right.'

'And look; phone me later if you have any news. I won't say anything to Joe's grannie as yet. His father is due back tomorrow; I hope Joe puts in an appearance before then as there's enough trouble next door without any more being added to it.'

'Yes, Father, I'll go to the police now. By the way, how's Mother and the girls?'

'Oh, Mother's all right. She's in the garden at the moment and the girls are doing fine . . . You got her letter about Bill, I suppose?'

'Yes, Father.'

'Nice business that, I must say, appearing in court. Well, he'd better make the best of what time he has left. I'll be sorry in a way . . . But more of that later. Now do as I've told you and do it quickly . . . Goodbye.'

'Goodbye, Father.'

The police, thought Jonathan dolefully; he'd had enough of the police already, but there was nothing else for it. There certainly was a jinx on this trip. Only three days afloat and they had run into trouble from the very start.

It was four o'clock the following afternoon and *The Mary Ann Shaughnessy* was crowded. Sitting on the single bunk sat a Police Inspector, and next to him was Malcolm with Bill at his side. On the double bunk sat Jonathan and his father, and by the side of Mr Crawford sat Joe's father, and in the doorway with his shoulders hunched because of his height stood a uniformed policeman.

The Inspector was addressing himself to Mr Taggart, saying, 'That seemed our main hope, that he was with his mother. You are sure, sir, that he isn't?'

'Positive, positive.' Mr Taggart shook his head vigorously, then ran his hand round his pale worried face. 'Anyway, she's coming here. She should arrive somewhere around six.'

'She told you, you say, that she put her address on the letter?'

'Yes.'

'Then he could still be on his way to her.'

'It doesn't take nearly two days to get to East Croydon.'

'No, no, you're right there.' The Inspector nodded

slowly. 'But a lot of things can happen to a young boy to delay him.'

'I don't think my son would go to his mother without my permission.'

'You don't know what young boys will do when they are emotionally disturbed. As you said yourself, sir, he was upset at his mother's absence.' The Inspector now turned to Jonathan and for a third time in the last half-an-hour he said, 'Now think again. Tell me exactly what he said before he left the boat.'

Jonathan bit on his lip and the Inspector put in quickly, 'Yes, I know you've told me everything you can remember, but there's often some little thing that escapes the memory and it could turn out to be of great assistance to us . . . just think.'

'Well,' said Jonathan once again; ' he said, "If I'm not back on time mind, don't you leave the fat chop for me", and then he looked at Malcolm and said, "And don't forget, galley boy, to take the eyes out of the spuds. They watched my every bite yesterday." '

Malcolm nodded in confirmation, and not even the policeman smiled now as he had done when he first heard it.

The Inspector put his head on one side and looked down at Bill, and reaching over Malcolm's knee he rubbed Bill's muzzle, then remarked casually, 'You caused a bit of a rumpus up at The Royal Oak I hear. Gave some folks a laugh, but not everybody . . . Your trip has been quite eventful, hasn't it?' The Inspector's head was turned to the side now and his eyes were resting on Jonathan. 'Being moored near the reed cutter when it started up; and before that gallivanting down the river in the middle of the night . . . '

'We didn't.'

'But you were on the river in the middle of the night, weren't you?'

'Yes, but somebody had untied the ropes from the rond anchors, and the wind blew us off the bank. And what's more, sir, we knew nothing whatever about the reed cutter, only the fact that none of us had started it up.'

'All right, all right, no need to raise your voice.'

'He's got every right to deny the accusation if he didn't do it.' Mr Crawford was bristling in defence of his son, and the Inspector nodded and said calmly, 'Yes he has, but what I'm trying to say is, if there's a bright spark among a group, he's apt to get up to all sorts of tricks. I'm just wondering if your missing boy could have . . . '

'That's nonsense . . ! Oh, I'm sorry, sir.' Malcolm shrunk back a little from the look on the Inspector's face. 'What I mean is that Joe stayed on the boat with Bill here while we swam up the river, so it couldn't have been him, sir.'

'Well, I was just wondering,' said the Inspector, 'because if a boy is used to getting up to tricks, he could also be the type who could take off for a tramp on his own and not think of letting you know.'

'Joe wouldn't do that.' Malcolm shook his head slowly. 'I know Joe.'

'I may sound prejudiced—' Mr Taggart was leaning forward now towards the Inspector '—but as Malcolm says my son wouldn't do anything like that. He's got a sharp pithy way of speaking, and likes a bit of fun, but underneath it all he's very sensible . . . thoughtful and sensible; he was never one to cause trouble.'

'Well, you see, sir, we've got to examine every avenue. Now what I propose . . . '

What the Inspector was about to propose was cut off by a voice calling from the bank, 'Anyone there? I've found these; they may be of help.'

The Inspector rose quickly and, going from the cabin, joined the policeman on the bank, to be immediately followed by Mr Crawford, Malcolm and Mr Taggart. Jonathan, too, left the cabin but didn't get out of the boat; he just stood looking up at the visitor who held a letter in one hand and a bag of crisps in the other, and he listened to the owner of *The Night Star*, saying, 'We had moored above Denver Sluice and I was taking a walk along the bank. I was . . . oh, probably halfway between the sluice and the mouth of the Wissey when I saw these lying near a bush. It was an utterly isolated place, and there was the letter held down by the bag of crisps. Well, I read the letter and then I came up river as quickly as possible.' He nodded along the bank to where *The Night Star* was now berthed.

The Inspector, after reading the letter, looked at Mr Taggart; then handing him both the envelope and the letter, he asked quietly, 'Do you recognize the writing?'

Mr Taggart's face had turned deathly white long before he had come to the end of the letter; then pressing his teeth into his own lower lip to stop it trembling he closed his eyes and lowered his head.

'I'm sorry, sir, but this throws new light on the situation,' said the Inspector very quietly now. 'It would seem that the news of his mother taking proceedings for a divorce unbalanced him for the moment.' The Inspector now turned to Mr Leech and said, 'Could you show us the exact spot where you found these articles, sir?'

'Yes, yes, of course. It was near a bit of muddy bank where the cattle had churned it up, but I also left a marker by means of some driftwood to denote the place because after all one muddy place on a river bank looks much like another.'

The Inspector now turned to Mr Taggart and said, 'There'll be no need for you to come at the moment, sir, if you'd rather not.'

'I want to come.'

'And I'll come too,' said Mr Crawford. Then turning to Jonathan and Malcolm, he added in a low tone, 'We won't be long.'

Malcolm stepped down slowly into the boat and stood by Jonathan's side, and together they watched the group of men walking towards *The Night Star.*

Suddenly Malcolm made a choking sound in his throat and muttered, 'No, no, he couldn't. He wouldn't, would he, Jonathan?' Yet at the back of his mind he was recalling the day when Mrs Taggart had left home, and Joe had sat with him in the summerhouse near tears as he said, 'It's me grannie has done this. She's out to get them divorced; she even said she would. Well, if that ever happened I would die, I couldn't bear it.'

And apparently he hadn't been able to bear it. Malcolm turned his head and buried it against

Jonathan's shoulder, and Jonathan held him and patted him, but all the while he kept his eyes fixed on the men as one after the other they boarded *The Night Star*. Mr Leech was the last one to leave the bank and as he did so he turned back and looked at *The Mary Ann Shaughnessy* and Jonathan thought, 'Well, that's that.'

Jonathan hadn't realized that up to this very moment he had been pinning his hopes on Joe's theory that *The Night Star* and its crew were a funny lot and that in some way they were connected with his disappearance. But now the idea was as deflated and flat as a pricked balloon.

PART TWO

6

Joe tried to move his feet and the effort sent an excruciating pain up his spine. He was cold, he had never felt so cold in his life before, nor had he ever thought it was possible to experience the throbbing that was filling his head.

As the grey light seeped in through the space at the top of the window, where there was neither glass nor boards nailed across, he turned his stiff aching neck and looked at the figure propped up against the wall an arm's length from him. The man's head was hanging towards his shoulder, his body was turned slightly away, and his other shoulder, resting against the wall, showed his hands tied behind his back. His legs, close together and stretched out over the wet brick floor, were tied tightly at the ankles, and the rope leading from them, as in Joe's case, was tied to a large sack of grain. But this sack was intact, whereas the sack attached to Joe's stockinged feet had burst and the fermenting grain was spilling over the floor, adding a sour smell to the dankness pervading the room.

They would be looking for him. These were the words that Joe still repeated to himself. At first they had brought comfort to him, but now, although they ran through his mind they had ceased to bring any hope because he knew that if they were looking for him it would be around Denver Sluice where, as THAT DEVIL had said, the divers would be searching for his body, and when they didn't find it they would come to the natural conclusion that they were too late because it had gone through the sluice when the gates had been opened on the night he drowned himself.

This was the second dawn he had seen breaking from this wet and filthy cellar. They called it a cellar because apparently it had held the barrels when this place was an inn, but it was merely a room a little below ground level. But you only needed to be a little below ground level on the fens, Joe had found out during these last two days, to reach water, and he had sat on the wet stones for so long that the lower part of his body was numb, and he still continued to shiver though his head throbbed and burned.

His companion's head moved and he opened his eyes from a fitful doze and, looking at Joe, whispered, 'Been asleep, young 'un?'

'I don't know. I can't stop shivering, and my head's burnin'.'

With an effort the man twisted his body round until his other shoulder was touching the wall, and he peered down at Joe; then, thrusting up his head, he yelled, 'You there! Do you hear me, you in there?' He waited a moment, then again he yelled, 'Hi there! You!'

There came a sound of scuffling from the next

room and the door was pushed open and, in the dim light at the top of the two steps, stood Sloper, his face red, his eyes bleary with sleep. He blinked from one to the other as he growled, 'I warned you mind, I warned you what would happen if you raised your voice again. You'll have a mouthful of greasy tow to suck on for the rest of the day. I warned you; don't say I didn't warn you.'

'Shut your mouth,' said the man against the wall, 'and bring the young 'un something hot, unless you don't want to be brought up for murder an' all. He's cold to the bone and hot with it. Look at his face.'

Sloper came down the steps and peered at Joe, and his lips left his teeth as he leered, 'Hot, are you? Well, you should be thankful; you've got it both ways, hot and cold.' He kicked at some wet grain under his feet and added, 'An' if you want it any cooler I'll oblige any minute. If I had my way you'd be right cool by now, you young upstart.' He accompanied this last remark with a sharp jab of his foot against Joe's calf, and as Joe winced the man against the wall said slowly, 'My God, if I only had me hands free.'

'You'd what?' Sloper came round and stood by the man now, and repeating the action with his foot, only harder this time and against the man's thigh, he said, 'I've dealt with too many of your sort. "If only I had me hands free," he mimicked. 'That's what they say to the newspaper guys. "I would have done somethin' if only I'd had me hands free." And what would you do if you were free eh? I'll tell you, you'd sit

89

there, just sit there, your belly full of scare, Mr Williams.'

'Well, loosen me and see,' said Mr Williams grimly. 'But in the meantime, if you don't want your big boss to give you another slating ... SLOPER, you'd better see the young 'un's alive when he pays his daily visit, hadn't you? He wasn't very pleasant to you yesterday, was he?'

Sloper ground his teeth together; then after using his boot again he went out of the room, muttering darkly to himself.

When the door closed on him, Mr Williams looked down at Joe and said, 'He'll bring something; he's a white-livered rat, that one, if ever I saw one. And don't you worry, son; they'll be looking for you as they're looking for me.'

'How ... how long have you been lo—' Joe was going to say 'lost', but instead he whispered, 'missin'?'

Mr Williams screwed up his eyes as he looked up towards the light. 'Four days I think ... five. You know you lose count of time.'

'I wonder if me mam'll come looking?'

'What do you say, son?'

'Oh nothing; I was just thinkin'.'

'They've only got three more days left to complete whatever they are going to do. How big is their boat do you think?'

'Going by the length of *The Mary Ann Shaughnessy*, I should say forty-five to fifty feet.'

'By, they're clever. I must hand it to them on that point. I'd like to bet that the ballast in that boat is worth a fortune. And their bilges simply bustin' with cash and jewellery. And who'd think of searching a pleasure craft with such a nice man for captain?'

Yes, who'd think of searching a pleasure craft with such a nice man for captain? The thought made Joe more despondent still.

The door opened again and Sloper entered with a mug in his hand and, putting it down on the floor, he pushed Joe roughly around and undid his hands. But Joe couldn't move his arms to the front of his body for a moment because of the excruciating pain.

'I'll give you three minutes dead to get through that. An' don't try any monkey tricks. I'll leave the door open just to remind you I'm on the other side.'

'Look here. What about mine?' said Mr Williams now.

'You'll get yours at the stated time, not until.'

Joe slowly lifted the steaming mug of tea from the floor and sipped at it. Then when Sloper had gone from the room leaving the door open, he put out his arm holding the mug to his companion's mouth. But Mr Williams, shaking his head vigorously, indicated his tied hands with a movement over his shoulder, and Joe, quick to take up the suggestion, put down the mug and, leaning to the side, set about tearing at the tight knot on Mr Williams's wrists. His fingers were stiff with the cold and he winced as his nail tore down into the quick, but he had managed to get his finger inserted in one loop when Mr Williams suddenly swung round and leant against the wall again, and Joe, grabbing up the mug, put it to his mouth, and so hot was it that he almost

91

spat it out. But the sight of Sloper looming in the doorway made him swallow the mouthful of scalding liquid.

'Put a move on and get it finished or I'll dampen the floor with it for you. It might help to cool you down that way.' He gave a snigger, and Joe said, 'It's . . . it's very hot.'

'Well, you wanted it hot, didn't you? Get it down you or give it here.'

Joe kept gulping at the tea until the mug was empty; then Sloper, having tied his wrists again, went out once more, and Joe, looking towards Mr Williams, whispered, 'I'm sorry.'

'That's all right, son,' Mr Williams whispered back. 'But listen. Do you think you could try moving your feet just the slightest every now and again, because if you could get rid of more of the wheat from that sack you'd be able to bring yourself nearer to me then perhaps you could have a go at the rope with your teeth.'

'I can't move me feet at all,' said Joe softly.

'Just try, just a little bit. It would help your circulation an' all if you could do it. Go on.'

Joe tried. He put what strength he had into his legs and, stiffening his body, he pulled upwards.

'That's it, a bit moved. Go on, try again.'

Again Joe tried, and a few grains of wheat spilled from the slit at the foot of the sack.

'Splendid!' encouraged Mr Williams below his breath. 'Just do a little bit every now and again like that. Don't overtire yourself. And you mustn't get too much out at once else they'll notice, but just enough so that you could pull yourself nearer tonight.'

Joe stopped his exertions and exclaimed on a heightened whisper, 'The night? You think they'll not find us afore the night?'

'Now don't get agitated, son. Likely they will, but this is just in case, you see. And once I could get me hands free we'd be out of here in a brace of shakes.'

So every now and again for the next few hours Joe tensed his body and brought a few more grains of wheat on to the floor. And then, when the sun was slanting across Mr Williams's knees and Joe's ankles, there came the sound of voices from the next room, and they knew that the boss had arrived.

Joe's body stiffened at the sound of the low voice and he kept his eyes glued on the door until Mr Leech walked down the two steps into the room. Behind him came the bandy-legged man, and behind him Sloper.

Mr Leech was impeccably dressed as usual, and his face looked the same, pleasant and kindly, except for the eyes. And now their steely gaze surveyed first Joe, and then Mr Williams, then came back to Joe again, and it was to him he spoke. 'Poor little Joe,' he said mockingly. 'Poor little Joe who drowned himself because his mother told him she was going to be divorced. Poor little Joe who was so upset he couldn't eat his bag of crisps. Do you know where they found your mother's letter, Joe? On the river bank where you left it before you walked into the water, leaving all your footprints in the mud. The footprints clinched it, Joe, conclusively, because they were identical with a pair of shoes the policeman brought from your home.'

Mr Leech now took a pair of shoes from the bandy-legged man's hand and threw them down by Joe's side, adding, 'And if you're a good boy and behave yourself we might let you put them on again. Heroes always die with their shoes on, don't they, Joe? Which hero have you identified yourself with? Come on, tell me . . . Have you lost your tongue?'

'I . . . I'll tell you this,' stammered Joe. 'They'll find us afore long an' you'll get it in the neck, you'll see. You . . . you're worse than the lot of them you are, pretendin' to be a nice man . . .'

'I *am* a nice man, Joe. If I hadn't been a nice man I would have let Sloper here do what he wanted to, on the morning he found you snooping around.'

'I wasn't snooping, I've told you; it was an empty house and I just looked in.'

'And saw too much, Joe, too much for your own good. And I did my best to warn you and your two friends off before, didn't I? But you wouldn't take a hint. Still, I repeat, I am a nice man else at this moment your body would be at the bottom of the river, somewhere out in the Wash I imagine by now. You'll be interested to know they're still dredging the river, Joe. Exciting, isn't it? And your two friends . . . you'll be wanting to know about your two friends. Well, it's hard to convince them that you are dead, Joe. Do you know, we spent most of yesterday afternoon together looking for you, Joe? We went right up the Wissey, through the lakes to Stoke Ferry. And then you know what your friend, Jonathan, suggested? He suggested we should try the Brandon . . . wasn't

94

that silly of him? Well, a funny thing happened to stop him, because, after they'd had tea on *The Night Star* and went back to their little *Mary Ann Shaughnessy* – I still think that's a quaint name for a boat – they found that their engine wouldn't start. Something had happened to the lead of the self-starter and to their sparking plugs. Mr Murphy here—' Mr Leech now indicated the bandy-legged man '—kindly went and had a look at them, and found that two of them were badly sooted up, but what was more serious he also found that the spring contact in the magneto was broken. You see *The Mary Ann Shaughnessy*'s engine is a very old one, Joe, and lots of things can happen to it, unforeseen things. Well, your two friends were prevented from exploring the Brandon and so I went in their place. I went right down to Wilton Bridge, in fact beyond, and got stuck in the mud there. But who minds being stuck in the mud in such a good cause?'

'You're a devil,' said Joe.

'Thank you, Joe. I try my best.'

'They'll get you,' said Joe.

'Well, they could, Joe, at that. Within the next two days there is just that slight possibility, but we won't let them, Joe, will we, for as long as you and Mr Williams decide to stay with me my fears are at rest. After that, Joe, *The Night Star* will be heading for her summer cruise, and you know something . . . you will be on board, Joe; both you and Mr Williams will be on board. I told you I was a nice man; there's nothing crude about me like there is about Sloper here.' He cast

95

a disdainful glance towards the big bullet-headed man. 'He would have had you both dumped in the river straightaway. He doesn't think. I had to explain to him that the bodies might not have gone through the sluice gates but have risen to the surface. That wouldn't have mattered so much in your case, Joe, but when it was accompanied by the body of Mr Williams, well . . . people become inquisitive you know, people like the Police Inspector. They're apt to ask odd questions that seemingly lead nowhere, yet ultimately reach an uncomfortable destination. Now my way is much simpler, Joe; cleaner if you know what I mean. As I said, you will go on the trip with us but you won't know anything about it; you won't even feel being dropped overboard in the middle of the ocean . . . Now don't you think my way is better, Joe?'

'You're a dirty swine.'

'Mr Williams!' Mr Leech's voice was curt now. 'I would advise you to keep your opinion to yourself or my manner towards you mightn't be as nice as it is towards Joe here.'

'Manner? You . . . As the lad says they'll get you. Your type always makes a mistake.'

'I haven't made a mistake so far, Mr Williams, and I've been operating for a number of years so I'm not likely to do so at this stage in my career. For your information, Mr Williams, I'm a respectable citizen. I have a farm in Sussex, run by my manager who is a church-going man. I too go to the village church on Sunday when I'm at home. I also have a chain of grocery stores, small, but growing, and your load of cigarettes will aid the growth considerably, Mr Williams. In fact, your company has been very helpful to me over the past two years; it has enabled me to extend my business and also to purchase *The Night Star*. I tell you this, Mr Williams, because I'm so confident that you won't split on me.' He gave a low laugh, and it was echoed by both Sloper and Murphy. Then Mr Leech, looking at Joe again, said, 'Sloper tells me you feel feverish, Joe. I'm sorry about that, but feeling hot has its points, don't you think, the floor being slightly damp?'

Joe was now leaning back against the wall. The aggressive feeling had seeped from him; he felt limp and more than a little afraid. He did not for a moment doubt that Mr Leech was a clever man. Added to this, he was as crafty as a stalking panther. What chance had the boys, even the police, against a man like him? And who would think about searching this house which was five miles from the nearest road? He had only come across it because he had lost his way when trying to find a short cut back to the mouth of Brandon Creek. And it wasn't likely that a pleasure boat would stop because of the broken staves that had once formed a landing for the barges. A boat could pull in further along the bank, but that was a long chance as this wasn't an attractive stretch of the river, added to which it was thick with floating reeds left from the cutter. And should anyone ever reach the house there was Sloper to tell them they were trespassing on private property. That's what they would have said to him if he hadn't uncovered the safe from under a pile of rotten corn sacks. He had kicked them with his foot in passing and felt it come in contact with something hard, and just as he had exposed the safe he had turned to see Sloper looking at him.

Wearily now he watched them as they filed out of the room, when, Mr Leech going last, turned at the door and, raising his eyebrows and with an apologetic look on his face, said, 'Oh, I forgot to tell you, Joe, that unfortunately I'm having to see to Bill. Your young friend, Malcolm, has got it too firmly into his head that somehow you can't be dead, and he had the idea that Bill, who apparently has hunting instincts, might be able to trace you if given the scent of some of your belongings. He was going to put it to the police today, but I hope to see Bill before the police do, and I shall present him with a titbit . . . What a shame it is that cruel people put out poisoned meat for foxes and such, and poor innocent dogs pick it up. It should be stopped, don't you think, Joe?'

Joe made no retort. He felt too sick.

'Listen,' whispered Mr Williams urgently when they were alone again. 'He means every word he says. We've got to do our utmost to get loose.' He made a quick motion with his head towards Joe's feet, and once again Joe made a mighty effort to try and shake the grain from the sack.

Two hours later there was a wider patch of grain on the floor and it went unnoticed when Murphy, this time, brought their dinner in. He unloosened Joe's hands first, then placed to his side a plate on which were two slices of cold bacon, a piece of bread and a mug of tea.

Joe didn't say 'I can't eat it'; he just leant his head back against the wall and rubbed his wrists gently and watched Murphy unloosen Mr Williams before taking his seat on the foot of the sack of grain at Mr Williams's feet.

As Joe watched Mr Williams eat, his eyes all the while on Murphy, he knew that he was waiting for Murphy to come just close enough so that he could get his hands round his throat, but neither Murphy nor Sloper were fools. They never came near Mr Williams before telling him to turn his face to the wall, and should he hesitate, a kick from one of their boots decided him.

Murphy turned now to Joe and said, 'Not nice enough for you?'

'I'm not hungry,' said Joe, lifting up the mug of tea to his lips.

'Well, I'd be the same in your place,' said Murphy. Then, looking at Mr Williams again, he remarked with a sneer, 'And the condemned man ate a hearty breakfast.'

'I'm not dead yet,' said Mr Williams grimly. 'An' I'll give you two guesses as to who's to be the condemned man.'

'Shut your gob,' said Murphy, 'an' turn round.'

'I haven't finished yet.' Mr Williams took up the mug of tea.'

'Never mind about finishing, turn around.'

'Well, come and stop me. Here, take the mug away.' He held the mug up.

Murphy came out with a string of oaths. Then picking up the long curved shaft of a pick-axe that stood against the wall he approached Mr Williams, saying, 'Have I to tell you twice?'

Mr Williams threw off the last dregs of the tea, then turned his body as much as he could to face the wall, and he groaned aloud as Murphy, with renewed viciousness, lashed his wrists together once more.

After Murphy had left the room Mr Williams kept his face turned from Joe and he made no sound, and Joe, twisting himself towards him, whispered anxiously, 'You all right, Mr Williams?'

It was some seconds before Mr Williams answered. 'Yes, I'm all right. Don't worry.' But he still kept his face averted, and Joe knew the reason why.

After a moment Joe whispered, 'I'll have another shot at the sack,' and now Mr Williams turned his body more towards Joe and muttered, 'Try pulling your knees up.'

When Joe tried this, the effort caused an excruciating pain to shoot through his body but the result was worth it because the sack moved just the slightest.

'Good,' whispered Mr Williams, his voice brighter now. 'Have a rest, then try again. Keep at it.'

And Joe kept at it; so much so that within the next hour he had brought the sack of grain six inches nearer, and his knees were now bent upwards, but he viewed this achievement with something of dismay when he heard Murphy entering the next room again, for now he couldn't put his legs straight. Although he pressed his back as tightly against the wall as his lashed hands would allow and pushed his feet flat against the neck of the sack, he couldn't straighten his legs, and his altered position was the first thing that Murphy noticed. He stopped at the bottom of the steps and

100

said slowly, 'Oh, aye! Trying your hand are you, or your feet?'

Although Joe was in a very feverish state he still had his wits about him, and bringing his head as far forward on to his chest as he could he groaned, 'I've got stomach ache, I'm feeling bad. The pain's awful; I want to go somewhere . . . I'm doubled up with it.' He made a rocking movement with his body and groaned, and Murphy, coming and standing over him, said, 'Well, that's just too bad. You're going to be uncomfortable I think.'

'Will you let me loose for a bit?'

'You're kiddin'.' Murphy grinned widely now.

'I tell you I feel bad.'

'The youngster's tellin' the truth, you little squirt. He's bad, and if anything happens to him God help you.'

'All you succeed in doing is make me laugh,' said Murphy grimly. 'Squirt, am I? Well, far better a little squirt than a big nit. You big fellows, you're nothing but nits. Who but a nit would fall for the old gag of the distressed damsel who couldn't get her car to start? You carryin' a load worth three thousand. An' you'd been warned, hadn't you? But you couldn't resist playin' the big fellow to a dear little blonde . . . You make me sick.'

Mr Williams remained silent. He lay back, slumped against the wall now. The truth of Murphy's words seemed to have winded him, and Joe continued to groan and rock his body, but it had no effect on Murphy. He went out of the room and they heard the outer door bang which meant he was on the river bank again to act as watch.

101

Wildly now Joe began to tug at the bag. And such was his efforts that he made more headway in the following five minutes than he had done during the previous hour. Now turning one foot, he placed the other on top of it, then fell on to his right side, while Mr Williams pressed his back towards him as much as it was possible, muttering words of encouragement the while.

'Can you ease back a little more?' whispered Joe. 'I'm just about an inch off it.'

Mr Williams strained his body backwards and Joe stretched his neck forward, and then his teeth were on the rope. The rope was wet and slimy and when he felt his teeth grinding on the dirt his stomach heaved, but he kept on tearing and pulling, until there came a point when he wanted to let out a yell of triumph. The rope eased through the loop, and Mr Williams's wrists, one running with blood, pressed outwards, and then his hands were free.

Rising on his elbow, Joe silently watched Mr Williams bring his arms forward and look down at his discoloured wrists for a moment. Then smiling at Joe, he said briefly, 'Good work, son.' Following this he drew in a long breath, then bent swiftly towards his feet, and his hands were on the rope binding his ankles when they were arrested for a second by a noise under the window. It was a snuffling, sniffing noise interspersed with another sound like a cough, and it brought Joe's head up and a light into his eyes, and before he could stop himself he cried, 'It's Bill!' And then on a higher voice he yelled, 'Bill! Bill! Come on, boy. Come on, Bill. Jonathan! Malcolm! Here! Here!'

There was a racing of feet now and the door burst open and Murphy jumped down the steps and into the room. For a moment he stopped dead and looked at Mr Williams tearing at the knots in the rope around his ankles, then with a bound he had grabbed up the pick-axe shaft and was on him, and Joe screamed aloud as it came down on the side of Mr Williams's head.

Making hardly a sound Mr Williams fell over sidewards. But Murphy hadn't straightened his back from the action before he himself was screaming and clawing wildly at an enraged animal hanging on to his arm. The man's curses rent the air as he staggered round the room in an endeavour to shake off Bill's hold.

Everything had happened so quickly that Joe was stunned for the moment. Then, realizing that where Bill was, the boys wouldn't be far behind he put his head back and screamed again at the limit of his lungs, 'Jonathan! Jonathan! Malcolm! Jonathan! Here! Here!' And then his heart seemed to bounce into his mouth when he heard the footsteps racing around the side of the house, then across the other outer room, but when they came into the cellar, his heart dropped back into a lower depth than it had been before because he was looking not at Jonathan, or Malcolm, but at Mr Leech and Sloper.

When Sloper's heavy boot caught Bill a vicious kick in his dangling hind leg, he let loose of Murphy, and then pandemonium rained as blow after blow was levelled at him and he leapt here and there, barking and growling in an endeavour to evade his attackers.

In the middle of the mêlée Sloper dashed into the other room and came back with a revolver in his hand, and he was aiming it at Bill when it was knocked flying by Mr Leech, crying, 'Don't use that in here, it's too risky. Get that shaft and brain him. And try to do it quietly, or else we'll have the passing crafts stopping to investigate. There's two just gone up the river.'

As Sloper picked up the shaft Bill leaped again but Sloper side-stepped quickly and Bill's hurling took him on to the top of the steps and into the next room, from where he did not stop to continue the fight but raced out of the back door and along the river bank.

Both Mr Leech and Sloper were bending over Murphy now and Mr Leech was saying sternly, 'Stop it! Stop it! Your arm isn't off; there's only a couple of teeth marks.'

'Hy . . . hydrophobia,' stammered Murphy.

'Hydrophobia!' exclaimed Mr Leech scathingly.

'I'd better get to . . . to a hos . . . hospital.'

'You're going to no hospital; I'll burn it with caustic.'

'No!'

'Yes! Get on board. And walk along to the boat as if nothing has happened . . . Do you hear that? As if nothing had happened. And stay aboard until I come, but send Duffy back here, because we are expecting company. That hound will bring those other two snoopers running or I'm very much mistaken.'

'I . . . I thought you said you put paid to the beast.'

Mr Leech turned and looked at Murphy where

he stood on the first step holding his arm with one hand; then he looked away again, saying, 'I thought so too. In fact, I was sure I had. I saw him go in the thicket where I left the meat and I never saw him come out again.' He glanced at Joe now and said, 'Doesn't your friend Bill like raw meat?'

Joe said nothing, but he could have explained that Bill had almost been poisoned twice by eating pieces of raw meat he had found on the moors, so Malcolm had told him, which was why he would never touch raw meat. His diet was tinned meat and biscuits.

Mr Leech now went towards the prostrate man and, bending over him, put his hand inside his coat for a moment. Then looking across the room to where Murphy and Sloper were still standing he said, 'Why did you lay yourself open to this?'

'I didn't. He was tied up; I knotted him as tight as a vice. I don't know how he got loose, but he was untying his feet when I came in.'

'There's the answer,' Mr Leech now pointed to the spreading grain and Joe's bent knees. 'Our clever little friend here had only to turn on his side, lean over, and untie his companion with his teeth. That's what you did, isn't it, Joe?'

Joe remained silent. His head was swimming and he felt hot and cold at the same time. But the coldness now owed everything to the fear that was filling him. Not only fear of what was going to happen to him and Mr Williams, but what would happen when Jonathan and Malcolm, following Bill's lead, came to the empty house up the Brandon.

7

'There he is!' cried Malcolm excitedly, pointing through the evening light towards the brown-and-white dot in the far distance. 'Here boy! Here boy!'

As Malcolm and Jonathan raced down the river bank, over the field, through a gap in the hedge and across another field, Bill slowed his trot to a walk, and when they came up with him, crying, 'Where have you been, you devil you?' he sat down and gazed at them as they hung over him, the while panting from their exertions, and his pained look voiced his opinion of their recriminations.

'Wait a minute,' said Jonathan suddenly. Then kneeling down by Bill he said softly, 'What is it, boy?' And Bill, turning his head, told them what it was by licking his left thigh.

'Good Lord! There's a big lump on his leg,' exclaimed Malcolm. 'He's had a kick, or been hit by something.'

'Come on, boy. Come on, up,' they said gently. 'Come on back to the boat and we'll bathe it.'

Bill stood up but he did not make any attempt to go forward; instead he remained looking up at them for a moment, then slowly he turned and retraced his steps the way he had come, and as Malcolm called, 'This way, you silly ass,' Jonathan said quickly, 'Wait a minute. Look, he's turning round; he wants us to follow him.'

'You're right,' said Malcolm softly.

'Go on, boy, go on. But take it slowly.' Jonathan walked alongside Bill who was limping now and so was forced to take it slowly because of the pain in his hip, but nevertheless he led them unerringly across the fenland. First through two more fields, across a road, after which they followed a farm track that led apparently nowhere until it came to a ditch.

Many of the fen ditches were gruesome affairs, being wide and deep, their bottoms slimy with silt. Malcolm, deterred by the width from taking the jump, looked for some other means of crossing into the next field but found none. Then he was put to shame when Bill leapt the distance and landed on three paws with a painful yelp.

'I'll go first,' said Jonathan. 'Then you take a long run, and I'll catch you if you jump short. Don't worry. You'll be all right.'

Taking a long run himself, he landed on the far bank, and it was well he was there to grab Malcolm, for Malcolm jumped short, with the result that he sprawled down the black muddy face of the ditch, and he looked a sorry sight when Jonathan pulled him to the safety of the firm bank.

'You'd better get some of the mud scraped off you,' said Jonathan, but Malcolm, wiping his chin and the inside of his collar with his

handkerchief, said, 'No, look. He's still going on
. . . Jonathan . . . ?'

'Yes?'

They were hurrying after Bill now.

'Do you think . . . ?'

'Don't ask. I don't know what to think; just let's
find out where he's taking us.'

Two more fields and over hedges, scrambling
through small openings in them; through a narrow creek that had its own sluice gate; on and on
past resting cows and startled rabbits.

'Where on earth is he going?' exclaimed Malcolm
wearily as they jumped yet another ditch. 'He's
brought us across country, we must be nearing
the other river.'

'There, look! He's stopped,' cried Jonathan.
'And he's looking round.' He pointed to a clump
of trees, the first they had passed in their journey,
and near them some low bushes alongside which
Bill stood waiting for them. And when they
reached him they saw their destination. There,
some twenty yards beyond the trees, stood an
ugly stone house with barred windows and surrounded by a tangle of overgrown garden.

'Why, it's the house on the Brandon, that empty
one, you know, Jonathan,' whispered Malcolm.
'The river must be beyond. We've come right
across country to the Brandon.'

Jonathan looked down at Bill but spoke to
Malcolm, saying, 'Why isn't he going forward
any more? Why isn't he going right up to it?'

'Well, we'd better go and have a look, hadn't we?'

'No. Oh no. If he's not going ahead there's a
reason. We'll lie here and wait . . . and watch.'

'But it'll be getting dark soon,' said Malcolm. 'We can't help that; all the better I should say. But we're not going across that open space now.'

'Do you think somebody is in there?'

'Bill didn't get that injury to his leg by kicking himself.'

They lay down at the edge of the shrubs and kept their gaze fixed on the house, and when the light started to go Malcolm said, 'Do . . . do you think we should go and tell somebody?'

'Tell them what?' asked Jonathan. 'We know nothing ourselves yet. We'd look pretty fools, wouldn't we, if we went to the police. That's what you mean, isn't it?'

'Yes,' said Malcolm hesitantly.

'We'll soon know if there's anyone there.' Jonathan moved his head slowly, while stroking Bill gently with his hand to still his low and intermittent growling.

'But how, if we don't go and see?'

'If there's anyone inside they'll have to have a light, and if they show a light it'll prove another thing – that they're not aware they are being watched.'

'They wouldn't put a light on in a disused house, it would give them away,' said Malcolm.

'They could have one in a back room, for who's going to see it in this wilderness? And even if they did, are they going to bother investigating what might only be a tramp sleeping up for the night? We are miles away from anywhere.'

'How are we going to get back in the dark over those ditches?' asked Malcolm now, under his breath.

'We'll follow the river bank. There's always a path of sorts along it. I'm not worrying about getting back; I'm worried about what we are going to find over there. There's something or someone in there, I'm sure of it now. Just look at him.' He motioned down to Bill. 'He's all bristles and raring to go now. It's as if he was waiting for the dark.'

The light was almost gone when they moved from the shelter of the bush, and as they did so Jonathan cautioned Bill as he held on to his collar: 'Quiet boy, quiet. No barking. No . . . barking. Keep close behind me,' he whispered to Malcolm as Bill tugged him forward. 'And keep glancing around you in case anyone should try to jump us.'

The fence that once hedged the garden was broken down and gingerly they stepped over it and crept around the tangle of undergrowth until they came to a pathway leading from an outdoor lavatory to the side of the house. Here a wood shed with a corrugated iron roof had been built near the lower window. The window was boarded except for a foot gap at the top, and a pile of uncut wood reached almost up to the gap.

Malcolm, tapping Jonathan on the back, pointed to the wood, then the roof of the shed, indicating that once on it he could see through the gap and into the room beyond, but Jonathan shook his head vigorously and didn't stop to explain that such an operation would be much too noisy. At one point he stopped as a slight rustling sound came from the other side of the wall, but it could have been that of a mouse scampering over the

110

boards. Then they reached the back of the house, went past another boarded window and to a door that was slightly ajar.

Jonathan now turned his head and nodded at Malcolm; then putting his hand tentatively out, he pushed the door slowly inwards. When it made a grating sound they both stiffened and waited, but nothing happened. Then with a lift of his head to Malcolm, Jonathan, moving sidewards, entered the dark room, and Malcolm followed him; and simultaneously they were borne to the ground.

In Malcolm's case, he was knocked completely senseless for a moment, but Jonathan, kicking and struggling, put up a fight until he felt a blow on the head that seemed to wrench it from his body, and he was only just conscious of being dragged over a bumpy surface while voices, intermingled with Bill's distant barking, swirled around him.

But soon Jonathan was brought fully to himself by his arms being wrenched behind him while his face was pressed hard against a wet stone floor; then when his legs were pulled back until his body was like a bow he cried out aloud with the pain. Trussed up like a chicken, he was swung round and thrust against the wall, and so excruciating was the agony he was experiencing that his vision was blurred for the moment. Then his mouth stretched into a gape as his eyes met the gaze of a similar bound figure. Joe was looking down at him.

Joe's face was deeply flushed; his eyes were bright and his mouth was wide open, and from it hung a trail of dirty cloth.

'Joe! Joe! Why, Joe!' Jonathan's expression conveyed both pleasure and dismay, but Joe's face showed nothing but dismay.

A movement to the side of him brought his eyes from Joe, and in the flickering candlelight he saw another figure trussed up. He too was gagged, but his eyes spoke for him, saying, 'Why did you do it? You walked straight into them.'

Now for the first time Jonathan looked up at Mr Leech. He looked at him long and hard and he told himself that he was an utter fool; he should have taken notice of his inner promptings over the past two days which had pointed to this man being altogether too smooth. How had he, and he alone, found Joe's letter when the river bank had already been searched? He had wanted to put this question forward but it had seemed futile to do so when the police had accepted Mr Leech's statement. Oh! he groaned aloud now. If only his father hadn't gone back this morning, then he would have reported them missing. But now nobody would bother looking for them until tomorrow when they didn't arrive in Banham's boatyard.

The arrangement was, they should take the boat down the river tomorrow, then take Bill home to be in time for the court the following day.

Mr Crawford would have stayed with them for another day but he felt it was his place to accompany Mr Taggart home as he was in deep distress, as were they all. It was as if the thought of his father had transmitted itself to Malcolm for now, his voice high and squeaking, he yelled,

112

'Wait till my father gets you! He'll tear you apart, he will. He will, you horrible slimy beast you! And me sticking up for you . . .'

'Will I tie him up, boss?'

'Not yet. So you stuck up for me?' said Mr Leech. 'Well, that was very nice of you, Malcolm. I wish I could say that it would go in your favour but I'm afraid that's out of the question now.'

'You daren't do anything to us, you'll be gaoled.'

Malcolm edged himself across the wet floor towards Joe as he spoke, and when he was at Joe's side they stared at each other until Malcolm's gaze was wrenched round to Mr Leech again as he said, 'Of course I wouldn't dream of doing anything to you. What I'm going to do is invite you both to supper on *The Night Star*, and there I shall foolishly offer you some wine, and that will be the reason why you will inadvertently leave the calor gas on in your galley . . . I can assure you there'll be no-one more sorry than me when you're found tomorrow morning. In fact, I shall make it my business to take part of the blame for your sad end: I'll never forgive myself for pressing you to take wine at your tender age.'

'You! You wouldn't dare.' Malcolm's voice was trembling.

'Oh,' said Mr Leech softly, 'I would dare, but what a pity that, like Joe here, you won't know much about it. What I would prefer doing would be to ship you together with Joe and our dear Mr Williams here, who has been so very helpful to our cause, and put you all to rest somewhere at sea, but I'm afraid the extensive bilges of *The Night Star* are nearly full and they will

113

be overcrowded when two more pieces of cargo are added.' He wagged his finger, first at Joe and then at Mr Williams.

Jonathan, biting on his lip to stop himself from crying out against the pain in his back, saw Malcolm's lips tremble with the fear Mr Leech's words had aroused. The fear was in him too, adding to the sweat running down his face. Unless a miracle happened they were all doomed.

Then the way to achieve the miracle seemed to present itself instantly, for Bill's bark came to them from outside the window, and in a flash he gathered in a breath and yelled to the limit of his lungs, 'Bill! Bill! Go and fetch Poppa. Fetch Poppa!'

Poppa was Mr Crawford's pet name, and when Bill was young the boys had trained him to bring their father's slippers by saying, 'Go and fetch Poppa's slippers.' Now Jonathan knew it was impossible for Bill to bring Mr Crawford, but there was just the remotest chance that he would fetch someone to this place as he had fetched them. His mouth was open to yell again when a hand came slapping across it, jerking his head back and sending his senses reeling. Only faintly did he realize that Bill had not answered his command, but having jumped on to the wood shed roof by way of the stack of wood had his head through the end of the aperture above the top boards and was barking furiously.

It was when the hand came down and struck Jonathan once more that Bill, with a clawing and a scraping, drew his body through the open section and entered the room for the second time.

What followed took only seconds to accomplish. As Bill sprang at Sloper the man hurled himself over Mr Williams's legs and Bill landed on top of Jonathan but immediately returned to the attack again.

'Keep down!' It was a shouted command by Mr Leech to Sloper and Duffy. Mr Leech now stood in the far corner of the room with a revolver in his hand. He no longer looked the part of the suave individual for his face was dark and menacing. As Malcolm screamed out a protest, the sound of the report reverberated round the room and, threading it, a pitiful yelp from Bill as the bullet whisked through his ear. Then followed a terrible silence as Joe without making any sound at all slumped sideways.

Mr Leech, the smoking revolver in his hand, looked to where the blood was staining the neck of Joe's shirt, and he thrust out his tightened lips before he said, 'Well, he's only got himself to thank. If he hadn't come sneaking round here in the first place none of this would have happened. Anyway, it's better this way.'

'Do . . . do something. Do something!' There were tears in Malcolm's voice.

'Shut up you! Or you'll be next.' Sloper brought himself from the wall, looking round as he did so; then added, 'Where is he, boss?'

Mr Leech now looked into the dim corners of the room, but Bill was now nowhere to be seen; he had gone as quickly as he had come.

'He must have got out,' said Duffy.

'He won't get far,' growled Mr Leech, in a voice quite unlike his usual tone. 'Give me that torch.'

He grabbed a torch that was sticking out of Duffy's pocket, then ended, 'You stay here until I find him and finish him off.'

As the door closed on him, Jonathan yelled, 'Bill! Bill, go . . . !'

'Don't you know when you've had enough?' Sloper was towering over Jonathan, the back of his hand ready to strike again. Then he stayed it as the sound of a shot came from outside. A few minutes later Mr Leech returned into the room, saying grimly, 'Well that's that.'

'You got him, boss?'

'Yes. In the hind quarters. He dropped into the river, and went down like a stone.'

Malcolm, who had pulled the gag out of Joe's mouth and was now supporting his head, dropped his own head down until it touched his friend's and brokenly he cried.

Jonathan, too, was stunned and sickened by the news. Bill, that ugly, loyal, brave friend . . . that fellow, as his father called him, was now in the river. He screwed his eyes up tightly to stop himself from giving way and joining Malcolm. As he drew in one deep breath after another he heard Mr Leech say, 'Now get yourself along to that boat as quickly as you can and bring her back here.'

'But you told me to fix the engine, boss, you remember?' This was Duffy speaking.

'Well, if the men from Banham's haven't put it to rights, set to and undo your handiwork. You'll likely do it in one quarter of the time they would, but I want her here, and pronto.'

'But if I should be stopped coming down the river in the dark, what then?'

'You won't let anyone stop you, you understand? You'll be both deaf and blind until you berth her here. I want to get this business over and done with, and unless they insist I stay for the inquest we'll be well out to sea by this time tomorrow.'

'Roll on tomorrow then,' answered Duffy. 'This place is getting too crowded for comfort.'

'And you, Sloper,' said Mr Leech now. 'Tie the young squawking one up an' all, just in case he decides to knock you out. And that's possible.'

Jonathan watched Sloper move towards Malcolm, but he turned his head away when he saw his brother being trussed up with as little consideration as if he were a dead fowl. But he could not close his ears to Malcolm's cries, nor his mind to the utter hopelessness of their position. Not for a moment did he doubt that Mr Leech would do as he had said. If they had been at the mercy of ignorant men like Sloper, Murphy and Duffy, he could have hoped that they would have made a mistake somewhere along the line, or even been deterred by the consequences of their acts, but not so Mr Leech, for he was not only an educated man, he was a cunning, wily, polished and cool man, and it was the last two qualities that made him so formidable.

8

The second shot had caught Bill, as Mr Leech had said, but not in the hind quarters. The bullet had whipped off the end of his tail and sent arrows of agonizing pain through his body and a spurt of blood over him as he dived into the water. Stunned for the moment, he sank down until his paws touched the slimy silt which grabbed at his weight like quicksand. He was repulsed by the contact of the silt as much as a human would be. This, together with the urge to survive, brought him to the surface again. The current had carried him some way down the river and his head broke the water among a cluster of reeds, and he tore at them for support and, making a great effort, hauled himself up on to the bank. And there he lay exhausted, his head on his front paws, his ear and tail bleeding profusely. After a while he turned his head to the side and tried to quench the flow by pressing his ear into the soft ground, and spasmodically he made an attempt to lick the end of his tail.

After some time the black silty earth caked with the blood and staunched the flow from his ear and the pain in the side of his head eased, giving way to a numb feeling. But not so his tail. The feeling here was as if it was being held against the bars of a fire.

It must have been all of an hour later when he dragged himself to his feet and stumbled across the fenland in the direction of the boat. The going was rough and the jumping of the dykes too much for him, so he had to traverse their length until he found a plank bridge by which to cross, then retrace his steps until he picked up the familiar scent again.

When eventually he came limping to the place where the boat had been, he sniffed the ground then lay down and stared at the dark water, and once more he tried to lick the pain out of his tail.

He turned his head slowly when he heard the footsteps. They were mixed footsteps, human ones and those of his own kind, and when the bitch came up with a low growl and sniffed cautiously at him he made no response, but he blinked into the light that was flashing in his eyes. Then a soft hand was gently tapping his head and a man's voice was saying, 'What's this? What's this, old chap? I know you.'

The man was from a cottage some distance down the river. He had helped in the search for Joe, and he had talked to Jonathan and Malcolm about this very dog because his Flo, who was of uncertain temper, had taken an unusual liking to the bull terrier and had gambolled along the bank with him. And now here was the beast bleeding from both ends and, if he wasn't mistaken, from what he could see of its tail the end

119

had been shot clean off. That was no trap snip.

'Come on, boy,' he said gently. 'Come on.'

Bill pulled himself slowly to his feet, but he did not follow the man along the bank; instead he walked into the dark, and then the light shone on him again and the man said, 'Not that way, boy, not that way. Come on home and I'll fix you up, then I'll find out what this is all about.'

But Bill still stood, and when the man came up and bent down to him Bill put out his tongue and licked his hand, then turned away and walked into the darkness again.

Standing still, the man watched him through the light of the torch, and when Bill stopped once more to see if he was following he shook his head. He knew the way of animals; he had dealt with them all his life. This beast was trying to lead him somewhere over the fens, but it was no place to walk in the dead of the night, so saying 'Stay boy! Stay!' he approached Bill and, picking him up in his arms with no protest whatsoever from Bill now, he retraced his footsteps along the bank and to his home.

But when once he entered his house Bill would have none of it. Although weak on his legs he stood scratching at the door until the man's wife said, 'Let him out; you can see he wants to go some place.'

'And I'm going some place,' said the man tersely. 'I'm going to get on to the phone to the police. I don't like this at all. This beast has been shot, and the boys' boat has gone from along the river. It was there two hours ago, I'll swear.'

120

'Well, you'd better take him along with you; he'll go mad if he's left in here,' said the woman.

A few minutes later the man stood in the telephone kiosk on the main road while Bill lay outside the door waiting. After the man had explained to the police about Bill and the condition he was in, also the disappearance of the boat from the bank, the station officer asked where he was, and when he told him he was asked to stay exactly there and a patrol car would be with him in a few minutes.

And it was only a few minutes before the patrol car came to a stop outside the kiosk, and two policemen got out. The policemen, too, knew Bill, as they had also helped in the search for Joe, and they looked from him to the man as he said, 'Those boys were bats about this animal; I can't imagine them going off and leaving him, in fact I wouldn't believe it for a minute. I don't know what's happened but the whole thing seems fishy to me. We'd better check it out – and get this fellow to a vet.'

'That boat going down the river in the dark, turning into the Brandon.' One policeman was looking at the other now. 'You remember? I remarked then that it looked like the boys' boat, and didn't I say they were leaving it late and looking for more trouble being on the river in the dark?'

'Yes.' The other policeman nodded, then said to the man, 'Thank you very much; we'll look into this.' And turning to Bill he said, 'Come on, boy, get in.' He opened the back of the car, but again Bill would have none of it. However he was in no condition to resist for long and he found himself being lifted on to the back seat.

'You'll let me know what's happened?' said the man.

'As soon as we find out we'll let you know,' said one of the policemen. 'And thank you very much.'

The policemen did not find *The Mary Ann Shaughnessy* berthed round the corner of the Brandon near The Ship Inn as they thought they would, and so, flashing their torches, they went along the bank with Bill limping behind them. It wasn't until they made to retrace their steps that Bill stopped, then moved on again and stopped again, squinting up at them through the strong light when they told him to stay.

The policemen looked at each other, one saying, 'What do you make of it?'

'He wants us to follow him, I'm sure of that. Look, hang on here and don't let him out of your sight while I go back to the car and report that we are on the Brandon bank and give them the situation.'

The policeman who was left on the bank dropped on to his hunkers and called softly, 'Here boy! Here!' And after a moment's hesitation Bill came to him and flopped down wearily at his feet. The blood on his tail had clogged now, and his coat too was covered with blood and dirt, making him look a sorry sight, and the policeman said just that. 'Poor old chap, you do look in a mess; I wonder how you came by it, eh?' Soothingly he drew his fingers over Bill's back and Bill closed his eyes and rested until the sound of the other policeman returning brought his head up and to the alert again.

The policeman rose to his feet, asking, 'What did they say?'

'They seem to be on to something,' said his companion tersely. 'Ramsey spoke to Inspector Morley in the main office and then the Inspector got on direct to me. I think he's got a hunch; something to do with another boat. Anyway, he's coming out himself, and he's ordering two more patrol cars to come over the fens. Hockley from Ely will likely lead them because he knows the fens like the back of his hand, and he'd need to, to bring the car across here in the dark. The Inspector's making for Brockle's old house along the bank here. You know, the empty place out in the wilds that used to be a pub. He says we are not to go near it, just hang around until they come. From where we are now he says the cars should be there almost as soon as we are, so come on, let's get moving. Come on, boy.'

Bill didn't need any command. As if he had understood every word, he was already walking well ahead along the narrow path on the high river bank. Once he stopped and his front legs seemed to buckle under him, but before the policemen could reach him he was moving again, and one man remarked admiringly to the other, 'He's a bull terrier all right; he'll hang on till he drops. The more I look at him the more I feel that he and the Inspector are definitely on to something. You know, he's not unlike the Inspector, in looks I mean.' At this they both laughed.

It was some time later, after much stumbling

and grunting, that one said to the other, 'How much further for goodness' sake?'

'Another five minutes I think and we should see it round the next bend.'

But when they rounded the next bend, they did not see the house, which was shrouded in darkness, but they saw a light coming from a boat in the river. And Bill too saw it, and he was about to make his way down from the high bank to the lower river bank when the taller of the two policemen called softly, 'Stay boy! Stay!' And Bill, answering as always the command of stay, stood hesitating for just long enough to let the policeman get hold of his collar.

'Quiet boy! Quiet!' He crouched down on the bank, holding him while he whispered to the other constable, 'Go along and have a squint. Be careful, though.'

As the policeman went cautiously along the bank Bill struggled to follow him, but the man holding him whispered soothingly, 'There boy! There! All in good time. All in good time.'

A few minutes later the figure of the other policeman came scrambling out of the darkness, saying urgently, 'Come on, there's something wrong. The boys are asleep, or apparently so on a bunk. And there's that big fellow, you remember, from *The Night Star*, the one the Inspector thought he could remember but couldn't find any trace of in the files, well he's in there. He went into the galley, came out and looked at the boys, then went in again . . . Come on.'

Once the policeman had let loose of Bill he was away, running drunkenly down the bank towards the boat, and he had just reached the bows when a man pulled himself upwards with the intention of jumping off. Stopping in surprise for a moment, he flashed his torch over the bared teeth and bristling body confronting him and he muttered thickly, 'God! You again. He said he had finished you.'

'No, he's lived to tell the tale.' The voice coming out of the darkness brought the man's hand to the iron handle of the starter that was lying on the locker, and the policemen, now standing one at each side of the hatch, looked at Sloper, and one said, 'I wouldn't if I were you.'

Bill, scratching the earth and growling, was now making tentative dives to cover the distance from the bank to the narrow deck, but the bows were turned outwards, and in his condition he was fully aware that he would never make it, but Sloper didn't realize this, and it was evident that he was more afraid of the dog at the moment than he was of the policeman for, backing to the further side of the cockpit, he muttered, 'Keep that beast away from me, he's mad.'

'I think he's got reason to be,' said the other policeman. 'Somebody's been treating him rather roughly. Do you know anything about it?'

'Me? No; why should I? What you want?' he now demanded as the policeman, stretching out, threw his leg over the gunwale.

'Just to have a word with the boys.'

Sloper was now standing with his back to the saloon door and he said, 'They're asleep. They've had a tough day. They're asleep. Better not disturb them.'

'Well, I'm afraid we'll have to disturb them. They've deserted their dog. It isn't like them, is it?'

When Sloper didn't answer or move, the tall policeman flashed his light over him, saying, 'Go on inside.'

'I'm busy; I've got to get back on board me own boat.'

'There's plenty of time for that. We'd like a word with you. Open the door.'

Sloper didn't open the door; instead he did a surprising thing. He lifted his hands and cupping them over his mouth, he yelled into the night, 'The cops, boss! The cops! THE COPS!' Then punching viciously right and left he threw the policemen off their balance, knocking one over the engine top. But as he made a dive for the side of the boat and the bank there, confronting him was Bill, barking loudly now. The deterrent was enough to give one of the policemen time to recover, to grab Sloper's legs and to pull him down into the cockpit again.

'Put the bracelets on him,' gasped the tall policeman, and while he brought Sloper's wrists together the other man clipped the handcuffs on him and, dragging him to his feet, said to his companion, 'Now open that door.'

The policeman opened the door, and the next moment exclaimed in awe. 'My God! Gas.' Then, putting a handkerchief over his mouth and flashing his torch, he ran past the sleeping boys and into the galley, and there he turned off the two gas taps that fed the grill and kettle ring. Pulling open the cupboard doors he looked for the cylinder, and when he found it he found the valve full open.

Coming into the saloon again he flashed his torch about until he found the light switch. Then he shook first Malcolm and then Jonathan, but their bodies remained limp. After pulling down their eyelids and looking for signs of gassing he turned to the other policeman who was at his side now and whispered, 'They're lucky. The gas hasn't had time to affect them, but they've been drugged. Let's get them out of here and into the air.'

But as they bent over the inert forms Bill's barking suddenly ceased. A strong beam of light flooded the boat and a crisp-sounding voice came out of the darkness, saying, 'I've got you covered. Now do as I tell you or you won't live to tell the tale.'

The policemen reacted by moving slowly into the cockpit, but Bill's reaction was to scurry along the bank into the tall grass. He knew that voice. He connected it with the man who had aimed a small stick at him, out of which a ball of fire had come and torn off his ear, and the same stick had taken off the end of his tail. From his cover on the bank he lay growling low down in his great chest, and waited.

The voice said now, 'Put him over the side, and try any tricks and I won't hesitate.'

The policemen couldn't see the speaker, but when Sloper, handicapped as he was, went to scramble over the side of the boat one of the policemen made a grab at him, and as he did so there came a whizz of a bullet within a foot of

127

his head and the voice said again, 'That should convince you I'm not playing; it'll be on the mark next time. Now unloosen those bracelets before I count five.'

One of the policemen took the keys from his pocket, and making a pretence of unloosening Sloper he pulled him sharply round and holding him as a shield shouted, 'Go on then, shoot!'

There was silence from the bank for a moment; then the voice came from another position, saying, 'From where I'm standing now I can see one of the boys plainly. I'll give you another five and then I'll shoot.'

The voice from the bank had only reached three when the policeman called, 'He's loose, but neither of you will be loose for long, the place is surrounded. Don't think you'll get away.'

As Sloper scrambled ashore the voice came again. 'I've got a surprise for you,' it was saying. 'If you're hoping for assistance from the fens you're going to be disappointed. We saw to the wooden bridge some time ago. Any car attempting to cross it would find itself in a rather deep and dangerous dyke.'

The voice, now addressing Sloper, became brisk. 'Pull up the rond anchors and take the tie ropes off the cleats, and push her well out into the river . . . No doubt you can swim, coppers.' The voice came at them now. 'But a couple of bullets below the watermark will keep you busy saving the occupants, and by the time you reach the bank again you'll find everything on the fenland quiet once more.'

Quickly Sloper obeyed the orders, and *The*

Mary Ann Shaughnessy left the bank, swaying a little as Sloper pushed at her bows with the boat-hook, and within a minute or so she was making for the middle of the river. As her bows swung away from the torch the tall policeman, tearing off his uniform jacket and crouching down to loosen his boots, whispered hoarsely, 'Get your things off, Arthur, quick!' And the other policeman was in the act of unloosening his shoe laces when the promised bullet hit the boat, shuddering her for a moment but spurring the policemen to greater efforts to be rid of their clothes. It was as the tall policeman raised his head cautiously above the gunwale that they heard the dreadful growl followed by a scream, and this was followed by a spate of frantic broken orders, 'Sloper! Sloper! . . . the gun. Get it . . . get him!'

'The dog's ɡ t him,' exclaimed the tall policeman excitedly. 'Look! You stay aboard; you can't drift far, there's no wind. I'll swim ashore and with the help of that dog I may be able to get them. Give me the bracelets and my truncheon.'

As he pushed the handcuffs and truncheon into his back pocket the other man asked, 'What if she sinks?'

'She won't go that fast with one bullet hole. There should be a bilge pump around here somewhere. Find it and, if it's filling, start pumping.'

As the tall policeman dropped quietly over the side of the boat and into the water, saying, 'Listen to that; he must be still hanging on,' the other one said to him, 'Be careful now. It's not just fun and games with those fellows.'

There was no answer to this advice except the

129

soft splash of the water and all the while the yelling and cursing coming from the bank and the frenzied command of 'Grab him! Grab him!'

Sloper, falling and stumbling on the steep bank in the dark, found it impossible to obey this order, for Bill was clinging to Mr Leech's shoulder and, as the enraged and now frightened man swung round, Bill swung with him. The only chance Sloper would have had of doing Bill further injury would have been if his master had stood still for a moment, but you don't stand still with a bull terrier's jaws clamped on the thick of your neck, and his legs clawing at your back.

His torch and gun gone, Mr Leech, at the mercy of the enraged animal, seemed to go mad. At last, in desperation he stumbled down the bank and flung himself into the river. Down he plunged but when he surfaced again his companion was still with him.

He was holding on to the bank and repeating the process when the policeman scrambled from the water only a few yards away. The policeman did not stop to attend to this part of the situation for from what he could hear the bull terrier was doing very nicely. It was the other fellow he had to tackle, and he was directed to him by his grunts and muttered curses as he searched in vain for the gun and the torch.

Sloper did not hear the policeman's approach until the man was almost on top of him, and when straightening up, he discerned the dark bulk towering over him he brought his fist with lightning speed towards the policeman's stomach. But the blow, although it reached its target, did not carry its full force because the truncheon had brought him a glancing blow on the shoulder, and when it came down for a second time on the side of his head his bulky body doubled up slowly to lie in a heap on the bank.

The policeman bent over double for a moment as he tried to ease the pain of the blow, and as he did so there came to him the sound of running footsteps, and, crouching down near the recumbent body of Sloper, he waited. He didn't know how many more there were but he felt he could deal with them one at a time. When they were some yards from him the footsteps divided, some going down the bank to where Mr Leech was still shouting from the river, but without so much ferocity now; the others obviously moving slowly towards him, and when the torch picked him up he was standing poised with his truncheon at the ready.

'That you, Dyson?' The question was uncertain as the newcomer didn't expect to see one of his colleagues in his stockinged feet, minus his coat and helmet and dripping water.

'O-h yes. Am I glad to see you!'

'Who's this?' The torch picked up Sloper.

'One of a nice little gang, I should say at a guess. There's another one who's been doing some shooting. He's in the river. The dog's looking after him.'

'I didn't know the dogs were out on this job.'

'They're not. He isn't one of ours — but it wouldn't be a bad thing to recruit him. But here, help me to get the cuffs on this one and then let's get the boat back; she's adrift in the river and there's trouble aboard her.'

'Which boat is that? There's one lying up yon side of the house.'

'It's the boys' boat, *The Mary Ann Shaughnessy*. They are both on her, drugged. This one here—' he nodded down to Sloper '—was trying to gas them. Pike is aboard with them, and I'm not sure she isn't leaking.'

When they scrambled down the river bank there stood another policeman, his light showing up Mr Leech's prostrate body. The man was sobbing aloud now and crying weakly between sobs, 'Get him off! Get him off!' But apparently Bill wasn't going to be persuaded to leave go easily.

Constable Dyson, bending over Bill, stroked his head gently while saying soothingly, 'That's enough, boy. That's enough. Come on, let go. Come on now.' He went as far as to grip Bill's upper and lower jaws and ease his mouth from Mr Leech's neck, but this done he had to hold him in check.

Mr Leech lay still now, panting and shivering, and he made no protest when his hands were locked behind him and he was pulled to his feet.

'Have you been in the house?' asked Constable Dyson of the others.

'The Inspector's there with Taylor. They've caught two of them. Inspector sent us on here in the direction of the noise.'

'Arthur!' Police Constable Dyson now called across the river to where he could just discern the dark shape of the boat. 'You all right?'

'She's stuck in the mud over on this side,' Constable Pike shouted back.

'Is she leaking, do you know?'

'Not that I can see.'

'Do you think you can start up the engine?'

'That's what I'm trying to do now. I couldn't locate the petrol supply, but I've just found it.'

'Good!' called back Constable Dyson. Then turning to the other policeman, he said, 'Will you take him—' he nodded down at Mr Leech '—and his pal along to the house? And as soon as I get my shoes and coat on I'll come along and report.'

As the policeman pushed Mr Leech up the bank one of them said, 'We should have been here long before this but the wooden bridge across the main dyke is broken. I felt her going and just stopped the car in time, else we'd all have been at the bottom. As it was we had a job to get across. We pulled the car off and left her at the other side. It was a good job I knew my way about the fens or we'd have been stranded.'

'It was indeed,' replied Constable Dyson. 'This lot was prepared for all emergencies . . . except that . . . And the persistence of a bull terrier,' he muttered to himself on a laugh.

A few minutes later, when *The Mary Ann Shaughnessy* reached the bank, Constable Dyson had the rond anchors and ropes ready, and soon she was securely tied up. And now, boarding her, he looked down on the boys as he slipped off his shirt and got into his dry coat, the while thinking how lucky they were to be alive. Nor could he help smiling a little after the boys had been lifted to the bank as Bill squeezed himself between them and lay stretched out, licking their faces alternately.

'He's happy now,' he said softly to Constable Pike, who replied thoughtfully, as he gazed down on the boys, 'He's about the same age as my Tony.'

'Who? The dog?'

'No, of course not. The young one here.' And he bent over and stroked Malcolm's hair from his face as he murmured, 'They've been through something. Just take a look at the elder boy's face; it's had a battering. And his wrists, chafed to the bone one of them is ... How did that lot think they would get away with it? I bet they reckoned on a verdict of misadventure on them when they were found gassed. Didn't they realize that the marks on their bodies would have proved otherwise? Those blokes always slip up somewhere.'

'Will you be all right until I go and report?' said Constable Dyson now.

'Yes, but make it slippy; these kids need seeing to. And we'd better get this dog to a vet, too, fairly quickly.'

When Constable Dyson reached the house the Inspector greeted him with, 'Well, a busy night, Dyson.'

'Yes, sir,' replied the constable. 'And sir; the boys on the boat, they're in need of attention.'

'Well,' remarked the Inspector crisply, 'they are not the only ones. Take a look in there.' He pointed to the door. 'Mind, there's two steps down.'

Constable Dyson went into the room, and through the light of the solitary candle his eyes were immediately drawn to a policeman kneeling

134

on the wet floor supporting the bloodstained body of a young boy; then after a moment he lifted his gaze to a man sitting on a burst sack of wheat dazedly rubbing a hand up and down his arm. Following this, his attention was brought to the far corner of the room where two men sat, their identity made clear by the handcuffs that linked them together, and standing next to them, supporting themselves against the wall, were Mr Leech and Sloper.

The Inspector came into the room now and, standing over the policeman who was holding Joe, asked, 'How is he?'

'Pretty bad, I should say, sir. No sign of him coming to. The bullet must have gone straight through his shoulder. And he's very feverish.'

'He's been like that for some time.' Mr Williams's voice sounded slow and tired, and it trailed away as he ended, 'He was a plucky nipper; never met a better.'

The Inspector nodded slowly. Then turning to Constable Dyson, he asked, 'What's wrong with the other two boys?'

'I think they've been drugged, sir. And the big fellow there was in the process of putting the finishing touches to them with calor gas. We were just in time.'

The Inspector walked across the room and stood before Sloper and Mr Leech, and after surveying them for a moment he addressed himself to Mr Leech, saying, 'Somehow I had an idea we would meet up again, Mr Leech. You just stepped over yourself, didn't you, when you got the idea of leaving that letter on the bank. You see, I had combed that bank myself not an hour before. I make a hobby of walking along river banks, and you nearly always find something, but I found nothing that day.'

Mr Leech glared at the Inspector before saying, 'You'll have a lot to prove.'

'Huh!' The Inspector made a sound like a laugh. 'We've got enough on you already to put you away for a long, long rest . . . and we haven't been over your boat yet.' Then, his voice changing, he said thickly, 'You're a dirty swine to take it out on youngsters like this, but you'll pay for it . . . Mr Leech. Or is the name Bradford? And it used to be accompanied by a beard at one time . . . You know something, Mr Clever-sides? You can alter your face and even your voice, but there are certain turns of manner and speech that stick in the mind. Remember that for the far future when you are coming out next time and taking up another guise.'

Mr Leech said nothing to this, but as he ground his teeth together his jaw bones moved against the skin of his face which no longer looked suave. The Inspector turned from him as Constable Dyson said, 'How are we going to get them all down the river, sir? You can't get an ambulance up here.'

'How many are there?' The Inspector began to count. 'Three, four . . . and our four gentlemen friends, that makes eight. Myself, Taylor there, you and the other two outside, thirteen altogether. Do you think that boat could take the weight to the bottom of the river?'

'I think she might just, sir. She's a sturdy little

craft. She's got a bullet hole in her about three inches above the water mark, but we could keep the pump going all the way . . . But why not take the big one, sir . . . their boat?' He jerked his head.

'No,' said the Inspector definitely. 'I don't want her touched till daylight. If my guess is right we'll be having some important visitors looking over her, and they'll be making some surprising discoveries . . . Which reminds me, I'd better leave Taylor and Hockley on board her just in case these gentlemen have any friends in the vicinity, and that will lighten the burden on the boat. She'll manage eleven all right, I suppose?'

'Twelve with the dog,' said Constable Dyson smiling.

'The dog? Oh yes,' said the Inspector. 'Where is he?'

'He's on the bank, sir, and he's in a bad way too. Parts of his ear and tail missing. He was no beauty to begin with and this won't improve him any, but he's the gamest beast I've ever come across. If it hadn't been for him . . . well, I don't mind saying that I think our main prize would have given us the slip, sir. That dog hung on to him until he wore him down.'

'Pity dogs don't appreciate medals,' said the Inspector, then added briskly, 'Come on, let's get them aboard. Carry the boy gently, Taylor. And you see to Mr Williams, Dyson. And I myself will escort our friends. Get moving!' He now barked at Mr Leech and his gang. 'And fast! And take a good look at what you can see of the wide open spaces, because it will have to last you a long long time.'

It was a strange cavalcade that made its way along the high bank and down to *The Mary Ann Shaughnessy*. And when they boarded the boat they laid Joe gently on the single bunk, after which they bundled the prisoners into the cockpit. The Inspector came aboard last, leaving the two policemen on the bank to push them off and to carry out his order of remaining with *The Night Star*.

And so, lying low in the water, her old engine working violently against the unaccustomed load, *The Mary Ann Shaughnessy* went down the river again, and only one member of her original crew was aware of it, but only just aware, for he was very tired. Bill had never felt so tired in his life before, yet he knew he mustn't sleep yet, not until the scent that emanated from the bows was separated entirely from the scent of his three sleeping companions.

Half-an-hour later the ambulance men were careful not to step on the sleeping bull terrier lying on the floor of the ambulance.

9

'Look,' cried Mr Crawford. 'If that animal is
going to the Town Hall you can count me out.'

'Oh, Father!' Malcolm, Lorna and Jessica all
made this exclamation together.

'Never mind "Oh Father!" ' Mr Crawford tugged
violently at his waistcoat, adding, 'And that's
my last word on the subject.' He now turned his
head towards Jonathan, where he was standing
at the side of the chair in which Joe was sitting,
his arm in a sling, and nodding his head from
one to the other he added, 'And silence isn't
going to break me down either.' Then, swinging
round and looking at his wife, who sat with her
back to him looking out of the french windows
into the garden, he made yet another addition
by saying, 'Nor condemnation of any kind.'

'Who's condemning you?' Mrs Crawford turned
and faced her husband, her voice light and airy.
'I'm in entire agreement with you. After that scene
in the court anything could happen anywhere.'

'Yes, yes, that's what I mean. See?' Mr Crawford's
tone was slightly modified now and, turning to
his family again, he said, 'There you are then.
As your mother says, anything could happen

anywhere when that fellow's around. As I told you he's lucky to be here at all, and if it wasn't for all the flip-flap there was in the papers about him, that judge would have ordered him to be destroyed.'

'He couldn't,' Malcolm muttered under his breath, his eyes cast down.

'What!' exclaimed Mr Crawford.

'Well, he couldn't,' said Malcolm boldly now. 'Because he would have looked silly. The very fact that he hardly broke the skin of either Sloper or Mr Leech, and he hated them like poison, proved he wasn't out to hurt the postman, whom he quite liked . . . when he didn't wave a stick about.'

'That kind of reasoning is all very well,' said Mr Crawford sternly. 'But you forget one thing. People may not die from dog bites, but they can quite easily die from fright, and I'm telling you for nothing. I myself wouldn't feel the same again if that fellow got his teeth into me . . . and didn't even break the skin.'

'I wish I'd been there . . . I mean in the court.'

All eyes were turned on Joe now.

Joe looked smaller than usual, even thinner than usual, and much paler. A narrow escape from pneumonia and the loss of blood from the bullet wound had taken it out of him. But after three weeks, what everybody noticed most was a lack of his natural exuberance. The boys had tried their best, with the assistance of the girls, to bring back his old verve. They had talked about their adventure, they had tried to get him to bask in the publicity, but up to date it had been in vain. But now they sensed a spark of interest in his wish to have been present when Bill, after being on trial for his life so to speak, had, a short while after his reprieve, and in the very corridor of the court, once again exhibited his flare for 'hanging on'.

It had taken some time to convince the gentleman who had been waving his stick of the reason why Bill objected to such behaviour. Again it was only the fact that the whole town, indeed the whole country, was on Bill's side that had averted yet another court case. As the Chief Constable was kind enough to point out to the gentleman, Bill was, as had been acclaimed, the rightful hero in the Leech case, for Mr Leech had been playing on the public for years, successfully changing his identity when he got into a tight corner. Had it not been for the bull terrier, he said to the shaken man, it was quite within the cards that Mr Leech would have managed once again to bring off a coup; the biggest of his career this time, as the bilges and hold of *The Night Star* had shown, for there had been found in them the contents of two safes and three bank robberies, the money and jewels all destined for Mr Leech's other house in Spain. And, as the Chief Constable went on to ask, what was the hero of this affair getting out of it? An extra half pound of cooked steak a day – he wouldn't touch raw steak – but did that compensate him for the loss of half his ear and the end of his tail?

The gentleman, resigned but not soothed, had unwillingly let the matter drop, for as he said, 'If the police are against you, who is for you?'

Bill himself was very grateful for his extra rations. He had, just five minutes ago, finished a nice hunk of cooked lean steak, not a bit of fat to be seen anywhere on it, and he now felt at peace with the world. Life was good; it never had been better; everybody was wonderful to him, except the old man, and he would come round, he always did. He understood quite well that he had to put on a show in the house and make his position felt, but during term-time when he had to take him out for his own constitutional – he was apt to run to fat as big men usually did – they got along very well.

From where he was lying at Joe's feet he suddenly turned on his back and lay with his four legs sticking straight up in the air. This action, coming on top of Mr Crawford's tirade, caused a howl of laughter and Malcolm exclaimed, 'He's laughing at you, Father.'

'That won't do him much good, or anyone else,' said Mr Crawford significantly as he made for the door. 'Well now, I'm going to get ready and I suggest you all do the same . . . for mind . . . ' He turned about and wagged his finger at them all. 'I'm not hanging round and waiting for any of you. Half-past two the presentation is and we leave here at two o'clock on the dot. Now remember.'

'You have been warned.'

'What did you say?' Mr Crawford turned sharply once again, and Jonathan, shaking his head, said, 'Nothing, Father.'

When the door closed behind Mr Crawford they all started to laugh, but softly. Then, the laughter subsiding, Malcolm exclaimed dolefully, 'It's a shame. He's got a right to be there. We are getting all the glory and all that money and he's getting nothing.' Looking across at Jonathan and Joe now, he said seriously, 'It is a lot of money, isn't it. Can you believe we are really getting it?'

Both Jonathan and Joe shook their heads, and Jonathan thought no, he couldn't believe they were going to share ten thousand pounds, this being the total of the rewards from the insurance companies and the two banks.

There had been some argument at first as to the distribution of the money. Jonathan and Malcolm insisting that Joe take half of the rewards on the basis that if it hadn't been for him they wouldn't have known anything about Mr Leech. But Joe had said, share and share alike, pointing out the blatant fact that only because Bill was so tenacious was he alive today, were they all alive today.

So Joe had his way, but one thing they all agreed on, Mr Williams was to have a substantial present, as also was the man who had found Bill on the fens.

Malcolm, voicing the miracle of their survival, said now, 'Doesn't Father realize that we wouldn't be here if it wasn't for him? . . . And we wouldn't, old boy.' He knelt on the rug beside Bill and scratched his tummy. Looking up now towards Jonathan, he said, 'We should do something.'

'He says he can't go, and that's that,' said Jonathan.

'Mother!' Malcolm scrambled to his feet and went

towards Mrs Crawford. 'Can't *you* do something?'

'Only put him in the summerhouse.'

'That isn't what I mean, and you know it.' He shook his head vigorously. 'He's forbidden us, but you, you could get away with it; he's said nothing to you.'

Mrs Crawford bit on her lip and, looking at the girls, said, 'I think we'd better get ready; we don't want any more fracas.'

'Oh, Mother!' Malcolm hung on to her arm. Then he turned his head towards Joe, who was speaking to Jonathan, saying, 'What about that thing you said yesterday, Jonathan, accompli ... you know, doing a thing and asking permission afterwards.'

'Oh.' Jonathan grinned. 'You mean *fait accompli*.' He looked at his mother now and grinned. 'Could you do a *fait accompli*, Mother?'

'I'm having nothing whatever to do with this. Now look, your father said ... '

Jonathan was at her other side now, and the girls in front of her, pulling her on to the settee, and they joined their voices to the boys', saying to the effect that she could get round their father.

'But what can I do? You can't carry Bill in a bag.'

'No.' They all shook their heads. 'But Mother ... ' Malcolm put his mouth close to her ear and in a loud whisper ended, 'You could carry him in the boot.'

Mrs Crawford rose quickly from the couch, exclaiming, 'Malcolm! Just imagine. Just imagine what your father would say if that fellow—'

144

she thrust her finger down towards Bill, whose hairless eyelids were well back surveying her '—appeared out of the boot at the Town Hall, and all the people there.'

'A *fait accompli.*'

They all looked at Joe now and Mrs Crawford joined in the laughter. Then, cuffing Joe's head gently, she said, 'I won't do it. And it's no use any of you trying to persuade me, I won't do it. Now get yourselves away upstairs and get dressed. Go on, this very minute.'

'What about you?' asked Jonathan on the way towards the door.

'I'm ready,' said Mrs Crawford. 'All except my coat.'

'You smell nice,' said Malcolm, sniffing the air about her in the manner of Bill.

With a thrust she pushed him into the hall after the rest, then closed the door and slowly returned to where Joe was sitting, and lowering herself down towards the couch again she looked at him for a long while before saying gently, 'And how are you feeling now?'

'All right, Mrs Crawford, thanks.'

'Inside?'

Joe looked down, and under his breath he muttered, 'Not so good.' Then, quickly raising his eyes again, he whispered, 'Will me grannie be coming?'

Mrs Crawford surveyed her hands lying in her lap and she rubbed them together before saying, 'I . . . I don't think so, Joe.'

'Oh, well, that's something to be thankful for anyway.'

145

'I . . . I think, Joe, she may go back to the North again.' Mrs Crawford was still looking at her hands.

'No kiddin'! You mean that?' Joe pulled himself to the edge of the seat. 'Who told you? Me Dad?'

'He did refer to it in a way when he was here last week.'

'Oh!' He shook his head. 'If only she had gone sooner . . . Mrs Crawford?'

'Yes, Joe?'

'When, when she goes, do . . . do you think I could come, come and live here because if me dad's away most of the week it'll be awful on me own . . . ?'

Mrs Crawford, her eyes still cast down, seemed reluctant to discuss this matter further and said somewhat airily, 'We'll talk about that later, Joe.'

'Yes,' said Joe, nodding slowly. Mrs Crawford was kind, but she had four to look after, and that was enough, and not wanting to embarrass her further, he made himself smile as he said, 'Well, I suppose I could go to a boarding school or some such place; me dad'll fix it.'

'Yes, yes, I'm sure he will, Joe.'

'Do . . . do you think he'll make it to the Town Hall this afternoon? He said he'd try.'

'Well, if he said he'd try, you know he'll do his utmost to be there.'

Joe nodded again. Then in a brisk tone he made a statement that in no way seemed to have any connection with the conversation. 'Me mam came to the hospital every day for a whole week,' he said. 'And the first two nights she sat with me all night. I knew she was there, I knew all the time. The nurse said I couldn't have known the first night, but I did . . . I did.' His voice was high in his need and Mrs Crawford was saying soothingly, 'Of course you did, Joe,' when the phone rang, and getting up she said, 'Excuse me a moment.'

She left the door open as she hurried into the hall and Joe sat gazing through it. He could see nothing, or no-one, in the space and it was like gazing into the emptiness that was inside him. Everybody was so kind. He had been in the papers; he had been the instigation of capturing the Leech gang; and now he was rich; but . . . but it didn't mean very much because it did nothing to help the awful empty feeling inside of him. There wasn't even any comfort any more in the memory that his mother had come to the hospital every day for a week, because she had come alone. The two times she had come when his father was there she had walked out again.

He heard Mrs Crawford talking rapidly on the phone and then she came to the living-room door, smiled at him, then turned her head towards the stairs and called, 'Jonathan! Malcolm! All of you! . . . and Harold!' she called to her husband, 'Come here a minute, quick!'

'What is it now?' Mr Crawford came to the top of the stairs, surrounded by the family, all in a state of undress, and she cried up to them, 'What do you think? That was Uncle Tom on the phone and he's selling *The Mary Ann Shaughnessy*. I . . . I don't know if I've done right, but I asked

147

him not to go ahead until he heard from us. Wouldn't it be wonderful if you bought her? I mean you Joe, and you Jonathan and Malcolm ... and, if you like, we ... we could have a share, couldn't we, Father?'

Jonathan came slowly down the stairs fastening his tie. 'Buy *The Mary Ann!*' he said under his breath. 'Good Lord! Buy *The Mary Ann!*' His voice rose higher and Malcolm, bounding past him, jumped the last three steps into the hall and dashed for the living room, crying, 'Joe! Joe! Did you hear that? What do you think, us owning *The Mary Ann!*'

'Great!' said Joe in an awe-filled voice. 'Oh, that would be great.'

'Now wait a minute. WAIT A MINUTE.' Mr Crawford now descended from the last stair, holding up a cautionary hand. 'Don't jump into this thing blindly. It's all right buying a boat, but it's what it costs to run it.'

'We could help with the cost,' put in Mrs Crawford eagerly. 'You did talk of looking for a country cottage to spend our holidays in; you said it would be much cheaper than hotels.'

'Now stop it! Stop it, Jane. Don't go pushing them into this thing.'

'I'm not.' She was laughing widely as she shook her head. 'I'm pushing *myself* into it; I feel I would like a holiday on *The Mary Ann Shaughnessy*.'

'Good for you, Mother.' Malcolm began to bounce about, and this was a signal for Bill to follow suit. A great roar came from Mr Crawford as he cried, 'Stop it! Stop it! the lot of you ... and you—' he

148

pointed at Malcolm '—put that animal in the summerhouse.'

At this moment the front door bell rang and Mrs Crawford, exclaiming impatiently but still laughing, hurried from the room and opened the door, and then, as she looked at the two people standing on the step she held out her hands, saying with deep sincerity, 'Oh, I'm glad to see you.'

When Mr and Mrs Taggart stepped into the hall she whispered, 'I . . . I didn't tell him. I didn't want to raise his hopes in case you might be late . . . or something . . . ' Her voice trailed away.

There was a quietness about Mr and Mrs Taggart. They nodded and smiled back at Mrs Crawford but made no comment, not even when they entered the living room.

Mr Crawford gave the visitors one quick searching glance, then crying, 'Hello there, John. Hello, Sally!' he added by way of a bellow now, which took in his entire family. 'Don't stand there gaping like stuffed ducks; I've told you what will happen if we're one minute late in leaving this house. I'll refuse to go. Get yourselves upstairs and finish your dressing.'

The girls and their mother, followed by Jonathan, went quickly from the room, but Malcolm stood, his face one wide gape as he looked at Mrs Taggart. He couldn't take his eyes off her, until another bellow hit him. Then saying, 'Yes, Father,' he glanced down at Joe, punched him gently on the side of the head and dashed out of the room.

Joe too was looking at his mother. He had never taken his eyes off her since she had entered the room. But not until Mr Crawford also left, closing the door behind him, did he speak. And then all he was capable of saying was, 'Oh, Mam!' before his face was lost against her shoulder . . .

Going up the stairs, Mr Crawford was still talking loudly, and coming to the top of the stairhead he turned and looked down at his wife standing in the hall, and he called to her as if she was at the bottom of the garden. 'Come and do this tie for me, will you?'

But Mrs Crawford did not go to her husband's aid as she was bidden; instead, staring up at him she said calmly, and quietly, 'There's not much time as you've impressed on us. What am I to do? Come upstairs, or take him—' she pointed a finger at Bill who was also standing at the bottom of the stairs looking upwards '—and lock him up somewhere?'

'Put like that,' said Mr Crawford testily, 'do you think I've any choice? By all means lock him up somewhere.'

And that's what Mrs Crawford did. She took Bill out of the house and locked him up somewhere.

As Mr Crawford had portended they were late arriving at the Town Hall, fully five minutes late, and when he and Mrs Crawford, the two girls, and Jonathan got out of one car they had to wait for Joe and his parents, who were accompanied by Malcolm, to get out of the other. The Taggarts' car had been obstructed by a lorry, the driver of which seemed quite ignorant of the fact that he was interrupting a public occasion, as the crowded pavement on either side of the Town Hall steps indicated.

The Town Hall steps, too, had its occupants. Four photographers had their cameras already poised, and at the top of the steps stood the Mayor, accompanied by two bank managers, a representative of an insurance company, the Police Inspector, and, to the side, Constables Dyson and Pike from Cambridge.

Mr Crawford, acting as marshal to his own party, pulled Jonathan and Malcolm together, and after reaching out and drawing Joe in between them, he looked for his wife, who just a second before had been standing near Mr and Mrs Taggart. But now she was not to be seen anywhere. She couldn't have dropped through the earth. But where was she?

Mr Crawford knew an agonizing moment of indecision. The mayoral party was waiting for their approach. Where in heavens' name had that woman got to! There was nothing for it, they must go forward. He gave Jonathan a slight dig in the back. But Jonathan, glancing over his shoulder, didn't move, not even when his father, bending his head slightly forward, hissed, 'Go on, boy. Go on.'

Then Mr Crawford's head was wrenched sharply around, for coming from behind the car, and trotting in front of her was 'that fellow'.

Never! She couldn't. She wouldn't dare. But she had dared. *Oh! Just wait. Wait until he got home.*

151

He glanced at her as she came to his side; then he glanced down at – that fellow, and that fellow, in his own particular way, smiled at him, and the smile said, 'Put a good face on it, old man. That's all you can do anyway.'

Bill felt happy, sort of hilariously slap-happy. He knew this was an occasion, in some odd way it was his day. He knew it before he even heard the people laughing as he preceded the company up the steps on which he paused only once when a man bent towards him with a square box held before his face. For a moment he had thought it was a stick and he made a warning protest in his throat but, after a low command from behind him, he trotted on again.

Malcolm, Jonathan and Joe simultaneously let out a long breath, as also did the girls and Mrs Crawford. But Mr Crawford still held his breath as he watched Bill approach the Mayor and Mayoress and the mace-bearer, and in a frantic second he asked himself if 'that fellow' would be able to distinguish between a mace and a big stick.

Unfortunately Bill wasn't able to tell the difference between a mace and a big stick, and that was how he got a front spot in the national papers all to himself. And that was why Mr Crawford never stopped shouting for weeks afterwards; and that is why the town is still laughing, and everybody knows that no matter what Bill does in future it will be no good reporting him, because people will just laugh and say, 'Oh, Bill? He wouldn't hurt a fly. He hangs on, but he wouldn't hurt you . . .

Yes, he'll just scare the daylights out of you. But didn't he lick the mace-bearer's face in an attempt to bring him round as he lay on the steps?' The reporters' photograph showed that plainly.

THE END